THE MURDER

50 PLUS CONDO BOOK 1

JANIE OWENS

Published 2020 by Gumshoe – A Next Chapter Imprint

Cover art by Cover Mint

ONE

RUBY MOSKOWITZ'S heels clacked on the concrete surrounding the condo pool, jarring everyone from their siesta in the sun. Several people raised their heads from their chaise lounges to see who was making all the noise. Ruby was ninety plus years old, decked out in her aqua bathing suit with matching heels. A floppy sunhat with an aqua ribbon belted around the crown bounced over her bright red hair.

"You're getting burned, sonny," Ruby said to a man lying face down on a chaise. "Your back's as red as the strawberry jam I used to make."

The man rolled his head to the side and saw who was talking. "Oh, my gosh," he mumbled, with his mouth tight, "how old is this broad?"

Ruby struck a pose and smiled with lips smeared heavily in crimson lipstick. Every pointed joint popped sharply toward the young man as she spun around to gain his approval. No one wanted to see what she was displaying. He turned his head in the opposite direction to avoid conversation.

Undeterred, Ruby clacked off, swaying her skinny self for all to view. Her overly tanned skin draped like crepe paper over her bones, wiggling like a puppy under a blanket as she sashayed around to find her own chaise lounge.

"Hi, Ruby, come sit by me." Rachel Barnes rose from her chaise to straighten the cushion in the vacant one beside her.

"Thank you, sweetheart." Ruby sat down, then swung her scrawny legs onto the chaise and leaned back to enjoy the Florida sun. "We're in heaven, you know."

"Yes, Ruby, we certainly are."

Rachel was used to Ruby's overly inflated impression of herself. She was one of the first people Rachel had connected with, idiosyncrasies and all, when she and her husband Joe had moved to the Breezeway Condominiums six months earlier.

Breezeway was a high-rise condominium designed for people over fifty, stationed on the beautiful shores of Daytona Beach. Each morning Rachel woke up to the sound of ocean waves crashing onto the sand. With a coffee cup in one hand and a newspaper in the other, she sat on her balcony daily and sighed with pleasure. Yes, this truly was heaven.

The couple had decided to retire to the beach instead of remaining in their four-bedroom house since their only child was busy with her own life and living elsewhere. They had decided that two people in their fifties didn't need a big house, so a condo had been the perfect option.

"You taking time off from the job?" Ruby asked.

She was referring to the management position of the condo that Rachel had been offered shortly after moving into the spacious apartment she and Joe occupied. Her husband had been a building contractor and plumber, so the condo owners had hired him as a maintenance man. He liked to keep busy, so it seemed like a good idea at the time. However, he rarely had a full day off with all the maintenance issues that routinely popped up.

"It's my day off, Ruby."

"Your hubby off, too?"

"Nope, he's working on Loretta's toilet at the moment."

Ruby gave Rachel an incredulous look. "You let him work in Loretta's apartment? I wouldn't. No husband of mine, and I've had quite a few, would be allowed to step one foot into her place."

"Loretta was a high-profile detective, Ruby, not a criminal, back in the day," Rachel said. "Joe's perfectly safe around her."

"I wouldn't be so sure. She may have acquired a few wrinkles and let her hair go gray, but she's still Loretta Keyes, the famous detective from Nevada."

"Those days are long gone, Ruby. She lives a very quiet life now, very low key." Rachel grinned to herself. She wondered if Ruby was jealous or just being ornery.

"Well, you just keep an eye on your husband, make sure he isn't hanging out up there."

Joe spending time with Loretta? Rachel hardly anticipated that ever being an issue. Joe wasn't exactly a hot dude. He wore a little roundness in the waistline and was practically bald, although he labeled himself as having thinning hair. In reality, it was a little more than that. You could almost read the newspaper from the shine atop his head. His face was ordinary and kind. He was quiet, gentle and ambled around as he kept himself busy. This man was not a womanizer. Besides, Rachel would know immediately if he stepped out of line, and he knew that.

Rachel had a way of knowing when Joe was going to sneeze before his nose even tickled. Some years back, she had known when he hurt himself with a sander, taking off a layer of skin on his thigh. She was in Orlando at the time, when suddenly a knowingness came upon her. Immediately, she dropped what she was doing and drove home. She found a note on the dining room table stating that Joe had driven himself to the emergency room. No, it was impossible for Joe to think he could step out of line and get away with it. Besides, he was also a God-fearing man.

"As far as I know, Loretta isn't interested in men anymore. The woman must be well into her seventies."

"More like eighty-six."

Rachel looked curiously over at Ruby. "She's never told me her age."

"She won't, but I know. Don't be fooled by the facelifts, that old broad is an antique!"

"And you know all of this because..."

"I know, that's all. And by the way," Ruby said, changing the subject, "You need to go to Macy's and get yourself a bikini." Ruby closed her eyes after that remark.

Rachel choked on her last swallow of Coke, then set the can back on the cement. "Why do I need a bikini?"

"You've got a dynamite body, girl, show it off."

"No, Ruby, I don't want to compete with you."

"Pooh and pooh," she sputtered. "You're a young thing, show what ya got."

"I wouldn't call fifty-two exactly young." Rachel didn't look her age. Her dark hair, although enhanced with color to hide the grays, fell straight to her chin, and the wispy bangs across her forehead accentuated her blue eyes, giving her a youthful appearance.

"It's young compared to my ninety-three."

"Okay, you got me there."

Ruby was quite the character, as were many of the residents here, Rachel had discovered. No one knew a lot about Ruby, except she'd been married and divorced a bunch of times, according to her. Rumors circulated she had been a fashion model. Considering how thin the old woman was and the way she carried herself, Rachel believed it.

Rachel could tell Ruby had purposely changed the subject, so she backtracked. "Why don't you like Loretta?"

"She was a detective. Makes me nervous." Ruby pulled her hat farther over her face.

Rachel wasn't letting go. "That's a convenient answer. There has to be more than just that."

"Nope."

"Loretta retired from that line of work a long time ago. She goes to church regularly. Why should it bother you that she was a detective?" Rachel rolled to her side and stared at Ruby. "Were you ever arrested by her?"

"How dare you!" Ruby erupted, sitting up and glaring at Rachel. "Why am I talking to you? Go somewhere else and sun yourself!"

"Ruby, I'm sorry. I didn't mean to offend you," Rachel said, pushing herself into a sitting position. "I was actually kidding. I'm sure you were never arrested."

"Well, okay." It was obvious Ruby did not want to confess anything. She lay back again, soaking up rays, saying nothing.

Rachel rolled onto her back. *Touchy old broad.*

TWO

"SO, are we set for seven thirty?" Eneida Sanchez asked as she stood by the office door.

"Yes, I will be at the clubhouse on time," Rachel said as she marked her desk calendar. "And so will Tia and Olivia. I already confirmed with them."

"Great! Then I'm off to work. See you then." Eneida Sanchez walked her round hips out the door of the condo's office. Blessed with generous physical attributes, her very curly black hair bounced around her pretty face as she moved.

Rachel and Eneida had hit it off immediately upon meeting at the pool, even though there was nothing obvious they shared in common. Eneida owned a no-kill animal shelter and was an active advocate for animal rights. Due to her devotion to needy animals and her children, there hadn't been much time for her husband. Consequently, they divorced quite a few years prior to her moving to the condo.

Although still involved with the shelter, Eneida was finally in a position to hire a man to do the day-to-day management of the facility after she was bequeathed a large sum. He lived on the premises where she once had resided. But now she was enjoying life on the beach and the smell of the salty air after so many years of kennel odors. She acquired friends at the Breezeway, one of whom was Rachel, and enjoyed her time off after so many years of relentless physical labor. Life was good.

"Good gracious! It's hot out there," Loretta grumbled as she slipped past Eneida and continued into Rachel's air-conditioned office with a check in her hand. "I don't remember Nevada ever feeling like this. It's just too humid."

Loretta patted at her coifed gray hair, which was done up into a massive bouffant with a twist in the back. A sparkly comb anchored the mass, and the aroma of hairspray wafted through the office. As thin as a dime and always appearing sophisticated, the elder lady was decked out in a peach colored pantsuit. Rachel couldn't help but think Loretta should dress lighter if she was going to complain about the humidity.

"I have the condo fee here," Loretta said, placing the check on the desk. "Your husband did a fine job with my toilet. It doesn't run all night and keep me awake anymore. I have such a hard time sleeping as it is, I don't need an aquatic serenade."

"I'm glad your sleep is no longer being disrupted, Loretta." Rachel made out a receipt for the woman. "If you have any more problems, please let me know. I'll send Joe back up."

"Thank you, dear. You're a darling." Loretta made her way back to the lobby and then into the heat of the day outside.

The phone rang. Rachel picked it up, half expecting to hear from Joe.

"I've had enough of those feuding fools next door! I'm going to call the cops if you can't hush them up." Penelope Hardwood didn't even state her name, deciding to just blast her discontent into Rachel's ear.

"What's happening now?" Rachel asked, knowing who she was talking to.

"Marc is yelling at the top of his lungs at Lola and she's screaming like a cat with its tail caught in a buzz saw. They've been going at it off and on all night and here it is, ten o'clock in the morning."

"Have you tried banging on the wall? Sometimes people get embarrassed thinking neighbors are hearing them fighting and then they shut up," Rachel said, offering her best suggestion.

"I've banged until my hand is bruised. That awful man is going to kill her. That's the only way there'll be any peace for me," Penelope said, followed by a deep sigh.

Penelope was a long-time resident in the condo. As Rachel's self-appointed confidential informant, the old lady kept Rachel up to date on all the happenings in the condo, reporting regularly on any inappropriate behavior of her neighbors. Her age now showed in her stooped posture. Wrapped in a sweater even when it was ninety-five degrees outside, Penelope seemed to always be at the right place when something was happening. Everyone knew she blabbed everything she saw and heard to Rachel.

"I'll come up there and speak to them. You stay inside your apartment, Penelope, okay?"

"Okay, I'll stay right here," she promised. "But you have to do something."

"I'm on my way," Rachel said, hanging up the phone and locking her office as she left.

Rachel took the elevator to the eighth floor. When she exited, she could hear the ruckus. Banging noises spilled onto the outside walkway, making Rachel think Marc was bouncing his wife off the walls. Lola's shrill screams split the air outside, followed by crashing noises, as if to suggest she was throwing breakables at her husband. Rachel wondered why no one had called the police. Apparently only Penelope cared what was happening in that apartment.

Rachel loudly banged on the front door with her fist. "Open up! It's Rachel."

Silence followed the demand, then the door slowly opened. Lola stood beside the door, her brown hair ruffled up and falling half into her face. A black eye had formed and the other lid was winking closed. The woman's nose was red from dried blood and her lips were swollen. Lola was a sight to behold.

"Hi, Rachel," Lola said casually, as if her appearance was perfectly normal.

"Lola, you have to know that you two are making a huge racket up here. I'm surprised no one has called the cops on you." Rachel stood back with her hands on her hips, looking sternly at the middle-aged woman.

"Oh, I'm sorry, I didn't realize we were being that noisy," she said, at first looking embarrassed, then her face split into a sheepish grin. "You know how it is, couples have little spats."

"This sounded like World War Three, not a little spat. Really, how can you stand there and tell me that? Don't you think your neighbors have ears? Most all of them wear hearing aids."

"Well, I don't know, I guess things got out of hand."

"Where is Marc? I want to see Marc right now," Rachel demanded. There were times she felt like she was running a kindergarten for elderly delinquents.

Lola's eyes grew wide with fright. Her swollen lips began to move but nothing audible came out.

"Marc!" Rachel called as she pushed past Lola, stepping into the entryway. "Come out here and talk with me."

The apartment was rank. *Pasta sauce? Sausage?*

A tall rangy man slinked from the guest bedroom and stood with a helpless look on his face.

"The neighbors are complaining about all the fighting you two do up here. This time it's really out of hand."

Rachel noted he was a bit disheveled. His normally slicked-back hair hung around the sides of his slim face, and his shirt was open, revealing skin. Bare feet peeked out under his jeans.

"I'm sorry, I didn't realize we were so noisy that others could hear us discussing things," Marc said.

Rachel didn't allow him an inch of excuse. "Discussing? I could hear you clear down at the elevator yelling at Lola. And she was screeching. There was no discussing going on."

At that point, Rachel let her eyes fall around the living and dining room area that flowed into each other. Broken glassware and food were littered all over the carpeting and dark smudges were on the walls where the two must have been doing some scuffling. Gouges in the wall were evidence objects had been thrown. On another wall she saw red marks that Rachel assumed were blood, or maybe pasta sauce. One chair was tilted on its side and a couple tables looked skewed.

Looking more closely at Marc, Rachel could see he had a cut by his right eye, a bloody, swollen lip and his left eye was starting to swell. He reeked of sweat and motor oil. *Must have been some discussion.*

"I'm appalled. Look at the two of you!" Rachel shouted. "Lola, you're a sight!"

The woman trembled as she braced herself against the wall. Her shirt was half ripped open and barely hung from her shoulders. One flip flop clung to a foot and her shorts were torn partially away from her body. A large bruise was forming on one hip and a jagged cut was visible on her forearm.

"You can't tell me this wasn't a bad fight; I can look at the two of you and see what happened here. And the neighbors have all complained." Rachel glared at the two as she shifted her weight from one foot to the other, trying to decide what to do next. "Look what you've done to this apartment! It's a mess!"

"We're sorry," Marc said, nervously rubbing one arm with his hand. The heart tattoo on his upper arm looked like it had an additional arrow crossing through. No doubt, Lola contributed to that cut.

"Yes, sorry," Lola mumbled.

"The Morgans own this apartment. They'd be furious to see it in this condition." Rachel was growing angrier as she spoke. "Is this how you two get your jollies? Is this some sort of a pleasure trip for you? I'm serious, is it?"

Silence followed, and then Marc answered.

"Well, maybe. Sometimes." He shuffled his feet around as he looked down. "But this time it, well, uh..."

"He got jealous," Lola interjected. "I think he got loopy from watching too many movies and then exploded because the grocery boy carried my bags to the car. He was in the car, waiting. He thought the boy had the hots for me."

Marc Rogers owned a motor cycle shop in town that sold all the accessories one could need. Rachel turned her gaze on the business owner who one would presume had some common sense. Maybe even an inkling of decency.

"Really? You got jealous of a boy? A grocery boy?" Rachel still had her hands resting on her hips.

"Sort of."

Rachel let out a big sigh of frustration, releasing her resting hands. "You two need counseling. Big time. I strongly suggest you get some professional help or I'll have to take this up with the owners of this apartment and the condo board. And maybe the police."

"We can do that," Lola eagerly said.

"Do it," Rachel commanded. "Immediately. I want to see proof that you're attending counseling sessions, or so help me God, I'll turn you in. This is your last warning."

Both of them nodded their heads enthusiastically, just like two bobble heads.

Rachel marched from the apartment and into the elevator. She was really looking forward to being with her friends. This had been a tough day.

THREE

"AGAIN? I don't understand why she doesn't throw that jerk out," Tia said. "I wouldn't put up with that behavior for one minute."

"Maybe she's partly to blame," Olivia suggested. "After all, it takes two to tango, as they say."

"Tango with me once like that and I'd dance him into jail," Eneida said.

"Another round," Rachel called out to the barmaid, waving her glass in the air.

The girls were drinking iced tea, their beverage of choice. The clubhouse in the condo was a great place for the girls to hang out, get caught up on the latest in their lives, and then not have to worry about driving home. Rachel didn't drink, except for maybe one glass of wine at a party, but that was a rare occasion. Even though the bar was conveniently located mere feet away, her friends didn't drink either because they had to work the next day.

Rachel added three packets of sugar to her tea and picked up a complimentary cookie offered by the bar from a plate, then took another one. "If he lays a hand on her again, I'm calling the police, although, it looked like she'd thrown her fair share of punches. Maybe they both need to go to jail."

Tia picked up her glass. "They both probably should have gone to see a doctor."

"Spoken like a doctor," Olivia said.

Tia Patel was a gynecologist. She had a sizable practice, but that achievement hadn't come without sacrifice. Born to wealthy parents in Haridwar, India, she attended college in the States, eventually seeking citizenship. Despite her independent nature, the Indian culture was important to her, so Tia honored her parents' wishes and agreed to an arranged marriage. But her dedication to her profession and the women she cared for over the years grew to become an unacceptable burden to her traditional Indian-American husband. They divorced after twenty years with no children.

"Here you are, ladies, round three. Hope it doesn't keep you up all night," the server joked as she walked away.

"I have papers to grade," Olivia said.

Sitting smartly dressed in a blue suit, Olivia Johnson's jacket fell open to reveal a nice set of pearls around her neck that contrasted beautifully with her flawless cocoa skin. Warm and loving by nature, the epitome of motherhood, Olivia had been widowed at a young age, yet managed to put herself through college with four kids in tow. She grew to become a good provider as a college professor at Bethune Cookman University and a role model for her children. Now that her kids were grown and gone, living in a condo seemed to be the perfect decision.

"Okay, what do you all think about me joining an online dating service?" Olivia asked, looking from one shocked face to the other.

"A dating service? You mean where you look at a bunch of men's pictures, read a bio and go," Eneida asked.

"Exactly."

"Not for me," Eneida said, pushing up the wrist length sleeves on her blue shirt.

"I don't think so, either. Who knows what nutcase you could encounter?" Tia said.

"Every man on those dating sites isn't a nutcase," Olivia said. "And I haven't had a date in twenty-two months, one week and four days."

"But who's counting?" Rachel cracked. She added another three packets of sugar into her new drink and picked up another cookie. "Seriously, that long?"

"Yes, that long. I would like to have a man in my life." Olivia cocked her head to the side. "And why not use a dating service? It's done all the time. Becky in registration at the university met a great guy that way."

"Well, if you want to try it out, go for it," Eneida said. "But if it blows up in your face, don't cry to me."

All three ladies repeated various versions of the same sentiment, wagging their heads to the side.

Olivia looked indignant. "What a bunch of party poopers! I was looking to you for support."

"We're just concerned about you, is all," Rachel said, placing her hand on Olivia's arm. "You are so sweet, you're liable to get your heart broken."

"But if I don't try, I won't know, will I? I might meet someone really special; we could fall in love and who knows where that..." and her voice trailed off as she wistfully fiddled with her pearls.

"Oh, there she goes, she's in love already and she hasn't even been on a first date," Eneida said.

"Eneida and Rachel are right; you're setting yourself up to be hurt," Tia said. "None of us want to see that happen." Sporting a spiffy pair of basic black slacks and a tailored white shirt, her clothes reflected her conservative, cautious nature.

"I'll be careful. I get to screen the men before I contact anyone, so that should weed out the phonies and bad ones."

"You hope," Rachel said.

"Let's try to initiate a positive attitude here, okay? I'm not joining the military and being deployed to a hostile country. I just want to go on a few dates." Olivia flashed a hopeful smile at her friends. "Lighten up."

The ladies looked around at each other and shrugged jointly.

"Go for it," Eneida said.

"Who's buying the next round?" Rachel asked.

"How many have you had?" Eneida asked.

Rachel grinned. "I lost count. Hey, I'm thirsty."

"You're acting giddy," Tia said, giving her a fishy look. "Okay, I'll get a round, then I'm leaving. I'm on call this weekend."

"Tia, why don't you date? You're attractive. You've got lovely skin, gorgeous black hair, you're a nice weight, men should be falling all over you," Olivia said.

"I work long hours. I don't have much time left after work. Most times sleep is more appealing than spending time with a man," Tia said, resting her elbows on the table.

"What's your excuse, Eneida?" Rachel asked.

"I've been thinking about it. I have more time now that I have a man living at the shelter. Jorge has taken a lot off my shoulders," Eneida said. "So, maybe."

"Join a dating service," Olivia suggested.

Eneida slid her eyes over to Olivia. "I think I'll try other methods first."

Rachel jiggled the key into the lock on her front door. She was trying to be quiet for Joe's sake. She really didn't want to wake him because he always rose early in the morning. And it was midnight. Joe would have trouble returning to sleep if he woke up now.

Feeling around on the wall for the switch, Rachel managed to light her path, but not before her heel snagged the throw rug by the door. It was intended to catch outside dirt, but it caught her shoe instead. She went down on her butt and fell back, her head striking the door with a bang. Rachel let fly a few choice words. She struggled to her knees and then stood up. That's when she saw Joe staring at her.

"Are you okay?"

"Of course, I'm okay."

"I wondered because it sounded like you were out here wrestling Rulon Gardner," Joe said with a deadpan expression.

"What? I was careful to be quiet."

"If that was quiet, I'd hate to hear the racket you'd make when trying to be noisy." Joe shuffled off to the bedroom. "See if you can keep it down so I can get back to sleep."

So much for sneaking in.

FOUR

"WHAT? YOU SAID CATS?" Rachel asked of the caller on the phone. "How can cats be noisy?"

Rachel listened to the explanation of how leaping cats can cause noise. Sometimes loud noises, it turned out, as if something had fallen. This wasn't the first time she had received complaints about the pets Eneida had in her apartment. As an animal activist and shelter owner, Eneida had a tendency to bring home animals. Sometimes that exceeded the acceptable number in the condo rules. And sometimes the cats didn't play nicely, or quietly.

"I'll contact her today," Rachel said. "I'm sure the situation will improve, Mrs. Donnelly." This was not the morning she would have chosen to deal with this issue, because she felt hot and a touch dizzy when she stood. She knew that Eneida was never receptive when it came to criticism regarding her animals. But Rachel had to inform her of yet another complaint. She caught Eneida by cell phone on her lunch break, purchasing pet food on sale.

"That old bat has nothing better to do than complain," Eneida said. "What she ought to do is get herself a cat. That would keep her busy and out of my hair."

"How many cats do you have up there right now?" Rachel asked.

"Umm, four..."

Rachel knew that meant she probably had eight.

"Get the number back down to four, Eneida. Do it today," Rachel said. "And how many dogs do you have?"

"Only one."

That probably was the truth. Dogs were harder to conceal than cats. Rachel knew of the Retriever-Poodle mix. He was a big boy, complete with yellow fur that shed in big clumps everywhere. The dog was older, didn't bark and loved everyone. The kind of dog that a burglar would be greeted by with slobbery kisses. He wasn't the problem.

"Okay, so please take care of your cat situation, Eneida."

"Okay."

Rachel hung up the office phone and rolled her eyes. She hadn't anticipated so much drama when she agreed to manage the condo. *Everyone seems to be a character, with few exceptions,* Rachel thought.

Then Ruby walked into the office.

The old lady placed her fists on either side of the red shorts she wore. With obvious annoyance, she pulled a non-revealing white top downward over her bony hips. Rachel was surprised to see Ruby dressed in ordinary clothes instead of her usual bathing suit.

"What's wrong?" Rachel asked.

"It's Penelope Hardwood again!"

"Now what's she done?" Rachel didn't believe Penelope had actually done anything wrong. Even before the woman opened her mouth, Rachel was convinced it was all Ruby, not Penelope, who was the problem.

"She's out there telling everyone that I'm an embarrassment! Me?"

"Now, Ruby, I'm sure..."

"That old bat dresses like Nanook of the North in ninety degree temperatures, and *I'm* the embarrassment? Really!" After speaking, she assumed an indignant pose, her eyes flashing.

"What is it with you two? Why can't you just try to get along with each other?" Rachel said. "Penelope is a very nice lady, sweet, retiring. She wouldn't hurt a fly."

Ruby's eyebrows rose."You're going to take her side again, aren't you?"

"It's not a matter of sides, it's..."

"You always take her side, never mine." Ruby turned to leave. "She's a busybody and gossip. I guess you like those types."

Ruby stomped from the office, slamming the door behind her.

Rachel rolled her eyes for the second time.

The next person to enter the office was predictable.

"Hi, Penelope," Rachel said, pronouncing every syllable slowly.

Ruby had been right in her description of the old woman. There she stood, a gray haired, slightly plump woman of advanced years, dressed in a plain housedress and one of her many heavy sweaters.

"Good afternoon, dear. I wanted to tell you about Alfred, you know Alfred..."

"Yes, of course, Alfred lives on the eighth floor."

"Well, he's not feeling too good," Penelope said. "I saw him weaving in the walkway and asked if he was okay. He said he was and went on his way, but I don't believe he was telling the truth."

Alfred Thorn was a very quiet man with barely any hair on his head. He usually wore a light- weight jacket, which gave him a formal appearance, at least for Florida. Given his proper appearance and manner, Rachel suspected Penelope was smitten with him.

"Oh, yes, Alfred..." Rachel started to say, but was interrupted. It seemed to be her day for interruptions.

"Of course, if Ruby hadn't been flaunting herself at him in the first place, the whole situation may never have happened. I suppose it's equally her fault," Penelope said.

"Flaunting? Oh dear." Rachel held her head between her hands as her elbows rested on the desk in front of her. "Ruby walks around like a mature former model. She wasn't flaunting herself at Alfred. Have you ever been to a fashion show, Penelope?"

"No."

"You might want to take one in sometime so you can observe how a professional model walks. It's the same way Ruby moves her body from one end of a room to another," Rachel said, looking up at the old lady. "She's not flaunting, she's gliding."

"I call that slinking. And it's unseemly behavior," Penelope insisted.

"In your eyes," Rachel said, trying to be patient with the woman. "Only yours. Everyone else thinks it's kind of cute for an old lady. But now Ruby thinks you're gossiping about her."

"I do not gossip. Never!" the woman said, raising her chin and crossing her arms over her chest.

"Then go apologize to her. Tell her you weren't gossiping behind her back."

Silence followed.

"Well?"

She released her arms. "Okay, to please you, I'll do it."

"Don't please me, please Ruby."

Penelope let out a deep sigh. "Okay." She turned toward the door. "But if she'd just not sway so much, maybe Alfred wouldn't..."

"Penelope!" Rachel was convinced the old lady was jealous of Ruby. And she needed to get over it.

"Okay, all right. I'll apologize. Good day." She left the office, gently closing the door.

I'm supervising kindergarteners. Old kindergarteners!

"And how was your day?" Rachel asked as she ladled cauliflower cheddar soup into two bowls.

"Nothing special. Do you want me to get the bread out?" Joe asked, walking behind her into the narrow kitchen.

"If you want some, I don't."

Joe gathered the bread and margarine from the fridge and took both to the table in the dining room. Rachel carefully brought the two bowls of soup to the table, then returned to the kitchen for her iced tea.

"Did you finish with that sink issue?" she asked as she sat down with her drink, taking a sip, then adding copious amounts of sugar to the tea.

"Yeah. Alfred seems happy now." Joe smelled his soup before he took a noisy slurp, then made a face when he found it was too hot. "He's a character."

"Only him? The whole place is full of characters."

"Alfred's a nice man."

"Yes. I think Penelope is smitten with him."

"Really? Senior romance."

"Penelope told me today she thought he was ill. How did he seem to you?" Rachel stirred the soup around to cool it before tasting it.

"Okay, I guess. He barely got out of his chair," Joe said. "The only thing wrong with him is he needs some exercise."

Rachel grinned. "Eneida has too many cats again. I had another complaint today about the noise her menagerie was making." She blew on a spoonful of soup.

"I'll bet it stinks up there." Joe shook out a slice of bread from the wrapper and pulled off the lid to the margarine.

"I shudder to think. I haven't been in her place in a long time. We always meet at the clubhouse. Or here." Rachel looked at her husband with a question in her eyes.

"What?" Joe stopped the movement of his spoon half way up to his mouth, returning her look.

"I don't know. I just had a funny feeling."

"She hasn't had any maintenance problems, so I can't go prowling around to see the condition of the unit."

"I know. Don't worry about it. Hopefully she'll return a few cats to the shelter and peace will reign," she said, spooning soup into her mouth.

Joe slurped his soup again and Rachel shook her head in response. That was such an annoying habit of his.

"How did Loretta's place look when you were up there?"

"Oh, very clean, neat. It was perfect."

"She has help come in to clean. Speaking of which, I wonder how the cleanup is going with the feuding Rogers?" Rachel put her spoon down at that thought and picked up the fan that was conveniently lying on the table. She began to vigorously move air toward her face. "You wouldn't have believed the mess up there! Broken glass everywhere and gouges in the walls. Blood stains, too. And *it* stunk."

"I don't like Marc. I don't trust him." Joe folded his bread in half before taking a bite.

"Me either. He's mean. And I don't know what to say about Lola." Rachel continued to fan herself.

"How about that she's stupid?"

"You got that right. I suspect she's an equal party to the fighting. Marc looked beat up, too. She might egg him on for an excuse to land a few punches to his face. Who knows?"

Joe shot his wife an annoyed look. "Why are you fanning yourself at the dinner table?"

"I'm hot. I shouldn't be eating soup. And it seems I have an issue with being overly warm lately." Rachel left it at that. Let him put two and two together. She was fifty-two.

"Hot flashes?"

"Yes," she reluctantly admitted. "It's okay, I'll just drink more tea."

"Humph. I'll try to be around the Rogers apartment tomorrow to see if I can catch any signs of cleanup," Joe said, changing to a more comfortable subject.

"Good idea. The Morgans would be horrified if they saw their apartment in that condition." Rachel put down the fan and picked up her spoon again. "I might have to inform them of the mess if that crazy couple doesn't straighten out."

A burst of thunder suddenly rocked the table.

"Here we go again," Joe said. "Right on time."

"I'll shut the computer down," Rachel said, rising from her chair. She walked down the hallway to the second bedroom where her makeshift office was located. Most every evening a storm rolled through during hurricane season, right at this time. It never ceased to amaze Rachel how punctual the weather could be.

FIVE

RACHEL DOSED off quickly for a change. Normally her nights were spent either attempting to get to sleep or trying to return. It wasn't unusual for her to wake at three o'clock and remain that way for two hours before she fell back to sleep. All the experts advised getting up and doing something instead of lying in bed. But they also advised not to watch TV or look at a computer screen, and even your phone. So, what was she supposed to do at 3 a.m., vacuum? Joe wouldn't appreciate that commotion in the middle of the night.

On this particular night, Rachel awoke at four o'clock. She tossed around for a while, then slid back to sleep. One of her special dreams occurred, the kind she couldn't forget as much as she tried. It was grizzly, with blood spurting from a woman's body, fanning out on the wall and streaking downward. Furniture was upended. Toward the end, the scene grew too dark to see any details. She woke with a start. After that, Rachel got out of bed, not wanting to chance resuming the dream if she fell asleep again. The blood she had seen was not a normal red, rather, a bright neon, and that peculiar shade kept flashing in her memory as she made her way to the kitchen. She instinctively knew the neon color was intended to signify blood. And murder.

Rachel made coffee, attempting to be quiet. She suspected Joe was getting up anyway. It was his time to rise, but certainly not hers. After a few minutes Joe appeared in the kitchen doorway, dressed in his normal jeans and a tee-shirt. "You're up?"

"Yeah, I had a bad dream. One of *those* dreams."

"What about this time?"

Rachel told her husband about the experience while he got mugs for their coffee.

"Who's the woman?" he asked.

"I couldn't see her face."

"Where did it happen?" Joe put some Stevia into his chosen mug, pausing to enjoy the aroma of the coffee.

"I couldn't see for sure because everything went dark. But I think it was in the condo."

His eyes flipped up, looking at her. "A murder in the condo?"

"Shush, don't give it energy. Don't talk about it."

Joe sat silently beside a small round table next to the wall, studying his wife. "You haven't had one of those precognitive dreams in a while."

"I know. And they're never about good news coming." Rachel added sugar to her mug before she sat at the table.

"So I've noticed. Usually someone dies."

Rachel nodded her head. "I wonder who this time?"

"I guess we'll just have to wait and see." Joe tilted his mug to his lips.

"Did you tell Penelope to apologize to me?" Ruby's face was flushed almost as red as her hair. She looked a bit disheveled, too, with her topknot askew.

"Why, did she apologize to you?" Rachel asked innocently, resting her elbows on the office desk.

"Yes. And you made her do it, didn't you?"

"I didn't say that."

Ruby glared at Rachel. "That's the only way she would have apologized, if you told her to."

"You don't know that. Penelope is a sweet, kind lady..."

"Who minds everybody's business," Ruby interrupted. "She's your spy. She runs to you with everything, most of which doesn't have any meaning to her and only serves to cause trouble. She's a tattletale. And a troublemaker."

Just as Ruby concluded her speech, Penelope opened the door. Ruby glared at her, then folded her arms across her chest.

"See? What did I just say? Penelope has something to tell you!" Ruby announced, swinging one arm out to point at the other woman.

Penelope paid no attention to Ruby, gathering her soft blue sweater over her housedress and focusing on Rachel instead. "There's a strange smell on my floor. I'm not sure where it's coming from."

At least this isn't a complaint about Ruby, Rachel thought. "What does it smell like?" Rachel asked.

"I can't say. My smeller isn't what it used to be," Penelope said.

"Maybe you're smelling cleaning products? That could be coming from next door. Lola and Marc are supposed to be cleaning up their mess," Rachel suggested.

"I don't think so. It's not a pleasant odor." Penelope glanced over at Ruby who had decided to be silent.

"I'll ask Joe to go up there and sniff around when he gets back from the store," Rachel said.

"Thank you, dear." Penelope turned her attention to Ruby. "She is such a sweetheart. Always takes such good care of us."

"Yeah, Rachel's a real peach," Ruby said dryly.

"Good day to you both." Penelope walked out the door.

"Now, aren't you ashamed of yourself?" Rachel asked, reaching for her bottled water and taking a long swallow.

"No. Next time she'll come in here and complain about my

bathing suit." Ruby stood with her arms still crossed in front of her. "She's vicious."

Rachel sighed deeply. "Anything else you have to say? Because I do have work here," she said, patting a stack of papers.

"No, I'm done," she said, unfolding her spaghetti arms. "Don't work too hard." Ruby left quietly.

Rachel began to attack her paperwork just as the phone rang. It was Tia.

"Olivia and I want to meet for drinks at 5:30. Are you in?"

"Sure. How about Eneida?"

"I left a message on her phone to meet us."

"Great. See you then."

Over their iced teas, she would have an opportunity to ask Eneida about her cat situation. Maybe that unidentified smell was from her overflowing litter boxes? After all, she lived just two doors down from Penelope.

SIX

"THE FIRST THING I want to know is, how's your love life?" Rachel asked as she accepted her tea from the server. The clubhouse kitchen issued a divine smell. Rachel's nose told her it was Toll House cookies coming her way. A big dish of silver-wrapped chocolate truffles, donated by Tia, sat right in front of Rachel. That smell was even more tantalizing than the cookies. It had been a long day and she was happy to be with her pals—and cookies—and chocolate.

"Well, that's why I wanted to meet for drinks," Olivia said with a teasing smile. "I have news."

"Tell!" Rachel demanded.

"I've been screening prospective dates online and found a couple I'm impressed with," Olivia said.

"So, you went out?" Tia asked. Obviously, she hadn't taken time to change clothes after work because she was dressed in a white jacket.

"Not yet. But I'm planning to," Olivia said.

"When? With who?" Rachel asked. "Spill the details."

"Tomorrow night for dinner. We're meeting at the Bombay

Grill," Olivia said, patting the side of her short black wig. Olivia alternated between her own short hair and wigs, especially during the summer.

"Oh, the place with the great Indian food," Tia said.

"That's the one."

"Tell us about him," Rachel said, slouching back in her chair and picking up cookie number one.

"He's multiracial, a doctor," Olivia said, nodding toward Tia, "and he's divorced. All adult children, so that won't be an issue. He lives in New Smyrna Beach and owns his own home."

"Is he cute?" Tia asked.

"Well, if a man can be called cute at fifty-eight, I guess he's cute," Olivia said with a grin.

Silence fell on the table as each paused to sip their drink and imagine what the good doctor looked like.

"Where's Eneida?" Rachel asked. Cookie number one disappeared.

"I don't know. I noticed her car wasn't in the lot," Olivia said. "Maybe she's working late."

"It's in the shop. Tires are being rotated or something. She's probably picking it up." Tia set her drink down and turned her full attention on Olivia. "Have you talked to this man?"

"Yes, we've talked, texted, and emailed. He's really very charming. Especially considering he's a doctor." Olivia sent Tia a wink.

"What's that supposed to mean?" Tia asked.

"He's not full of himself. He seems to care about people and is not in the business just to make money. Like *some* doctors, present company excluded." Olivia smiled broadly at her friend.

"He sounds okay. But don't put on any airs, be yourself," Rachel said. She reached for a pile of truffles and stuffed them in the pocket of her shorts. Then took a bite of cookie number two.

"What? Why would I put on airs?" Olivia looked shocked at the notion.

"I hope you realize that things have changed a lot since we dated back in high school and college, and not necessarily for the better." Rachel swirled her straw among the ice cubes, watching the cloud of sugar rise and fall. "Have you even been on a date since you lost your husband?"

Olivia drew herself up and looked down her nose at Rachel. "Of course, I have. I dated a lot after the youngest went off to college. All the kids were out of the house, so I was free to do as I pleased. I dated *lots* of men. Emphasis on dated, nothing serious." Olivia plunged her straw up and down in her iced tea. "You're forgetting, I said I hadn't been on a date in so many months."

"She did say that," Tia said, reaching back to check the condition of the bun resting on the nape of her neck.

"Okay, sorry. I just didn't want you to be shocked if the good doctor proposed a late-night drink at his wonderful home," Rachel said, taking a quick sip of her tea.

"I was widowed umpteen years ago. Of course, I've dated, and I know what's happening in the world around me. I'm not stupid." Olivia pulled indignantly at her jacket, sitting a little straighter. "Now, *you* would be the one in for a few shocks if you were on the dating scene."

"Probably so," Rachel admitted. "I can't imagine dating anyone but Joe. My sweet, considerate man."

"Ladies, let's order another round prior to draining our glasses," Tia suggested before the tension rose any further.

But Olivia wasn't done. "You haven't known me long enough to be aware of my dating history. It's just been a dry spell, lately. I don't seem to be finding the right sort of man that I want to date. So, I'm exercising other options," she explained. "I am very selective when it comes to whom I spend time with."

"Olivia, I wish you the best with your new man. But you're so sweet and motherly, I just don't want to see you get hurt," Rachel said, leaning toward her friend.

"I've done my homework. It will be fine," Olivia said.

"I'll have another," Tia said to the server as she passed nearby. "They want one, too.

"And another plate of cookies," said Rachel. She had eaten the entire first batch herself.

As the server retreated for more drinks, Rachel had a thought. "So, Tia, how's your love life?"

Tia all but choked on the last swallow of her drink. "Well, still nonexistent. And I'm not looking, as I've said before."

"Why not?" Olivia asked.

"I'm too busy. I don't have time to put into a relationship. If that had been my focus, I'd still be married!"

"I understand," Olivia said. "But *I'm* ready for a man in my life. I just want support from my girlfriends."

"You've got it," Tia said.

"Me, too. I'm in your corner," Rachel said.

"That's all I wanted to hear." Olivia shot everyone a smile.

When the drinks arrived, everyone toasted the new relationship for Olivia.

SEVEN

RACHEL CRAWLED into bed beside Joe. It was late and she felt sort of drunk. Truth be told, she felt quite inebriated, but she hadn't had an alcoholic drink all night. Just iced tea and sweets. So, why was her head spinning?

She tried to settle in for a good night's sleep, but was met with a rocky start. Finally, she was able to doze off, drifting into a peaceful slumber. But somewhere after 3 a.m., her dreams produced a bazaar scene. People were shouting and pushing inside a subway car. It appeared some were pushing to get out, at the same time other passengers were trying to jamb themselves inside from the loading station. It was a terrible crush happening before her eyes, with arms and legs flailing everywhere, even some sticking out the door after it closed. A screaming mouth on a man's face grew so big that it swallowed the whole scene. Rachel woke with a start.

Rachel's heart was doing the samba in her chest and she felt hot. As she turned her head toward the doorway, she noticed a mist and a figure begin to form within. From a few droplets, the image expanded in all directions until the elements took the shape of a woman. Rachel realized this was a spirit as it drifted closer to the bed, stopping parallel. The spirit had curly black hair waving down to the shoulders, and lips that were moving as if she were trying to speak, yet no sound was heard. Suddenly, she recognized who it was.

"Eneida!" Rachel sat upright in bed, staring. When the spirit spoke the second time, she heard her.

"I wanted to say goodbye."

Shocked and stupefied, Rachel's mouth was dry and hanging open as she clutched the bedsheets between both hands. She stared at the image of Eneida.

"What happened?" she managed in a low voice.

"I love you, my friend."

Then Eneida's spirit dissipated.

Oh, my heavens, was all Rachel could think. Realizing that Eneida was dead, suddenly gave her another explanation for the odor in the hallway that Penelope had mentioned. She had forgotten to ask Joe to go upstairs to find the cause.

"Joe!" Rachel's hand shot out toward her husband, punching him in the ribs as he lay with his back toward her.

Joe's eyes flew open and widened, the way any man would react who had been shocked from a sound sleep.

"Wake up!" Rachel frantically shouted, pushing on Joe.

"What's wrong? Is there a burglar?" Joe rubbed at his eyes and turned toward his wife. "Can't this wait till morning?"

"No!" Was the man crazy? "Eneida's dead!"

Joe looked at his wife in the semi darkness. From his expression, he didn't appear overly impressed or concerned by her statements.

"So, you dreamed she died...You can tell me all about it in the morning."

"No! She was just here!"

Joe looked blankly at Rachel, then turned his head in the opposite direction to read the clock. "It's three thirty. Which is it, she's dead or was just here? Make up your mind and go back to sleep. I am."

"I forgot to tell you to go find out why there's a stink in her hallway," Rachel said, shaking her husband while he attempted to return to sleep. "It's Eneida. I know it. She's *dead!*"

Joe let out a long sigh as he closed his eyes. "Good. I'll go smell around in the morning. She's not going anywhere before then if she's dead."

"I'm not dreaming and I'm not kidding around. And I don't want to wait until morning," she said, emphasizing each word. "We have to go to her unit — *right now*!" She started pulling at his arm.

Joe opened his eyes and swung his body from the bed. "All I can say is, she'd better be dead when we get up there or you're going to be the dead one for waking me up."

"I know you don't mean that."

"This better not be one of your dreams."

Rachel suddenly remembered her dream about the dead person and the neon red blood dripping down the wall. "Joe. The dream. Remember the dream I had?"

Joe stopped his parade to the bathroom just short of the doorway. "Oh, yeah. The dead body."

"It was Eneida I was dreaming about," Rachel said to his back.

"Let me finish in here and I'll throw on my jeans."

Rachel donned a housedress over her nightie and slipped on a pair of flipflops. They were out the door in three minutes, headed for the office. With shaking hands, Rachel unlocked the office door, located the appropriate set of keys for Eneida's unit, and marched to the elevator with Joe.

When they came off the elevator, the odor in the walkway was not pleasant, smelling like a kennel mixed with something else. Rachel handed Joe the keys for him to unlock the door. She braced herself for whatever scene was on the other side. When the door swung open, the unit was too dark to see anything until Joe flipped on the wall switch by the door. What met their eyes was gruesome.

"Oh, my..." Rachel murmured so softly that Joe barely heard her words.

"This is bad. I'll call 911," Joe said, pulling his phone from his back pocket.

All Rachel could do was stare at the scene before her, with lips parted and hands clutched together. Furniture was turned over, lamps were broken on the floor, and animals were peacefully resting in crates in the middle of the living room. Rachel immediately noticed the fan-shaped blood that dripped from the wall down to the floor. Exactly as in her dream, but not neon red. Something awful had obviously happened here, but where was Eneida?

"I don't see Eneida, Joe."

Rachel called out her name, but there was no response. She was actually afraid to walk forward, her knees trembling in fear over what she would see.

Joe gave information to the dispatcher on his phone as he walked toward the closest bedroom. "Cops are coming," he said, glancing back at Rachel. "I'll look in the bedroom for Eneida. You should stay here." He returned the phone to his back pocket.

As Joe went to investigate the bedroom, Rachel took shallow breaths, squared her shoulders, and walked toward the crates. She wondered how long the poor things had been cooped up. There were four cat carriers, but only three cats were inside the crates. The large crate was for the dog. *The poor dog must be miserable* was Rachel's first thought as she reached down to unlatch the dog crate. Glancing to the side, Rachel saw Joe and the dog come out of the bedroom.

"Found the dog," Joe said. "He's not much of a guard dog, is he?"

"Well I wonder what's in his crate? Something is in here," Rachel said as she pulled the latch open.

A bloody bare foot and leg sprang from the crate. Rachel screamed. Joe grabbed her away with a quick movement, holding her head to his chest so she couldn't look at the gruesome scene. Shushing the sobs that began, he rocked his wife in comforting arms and stroked her hair.

"Here, let's go into the kitchen," Joe suggested, drawing her through the living room and dining room, then into the kitchen. "Sit in the chair. I'll get you some water."

Rachel numbly tilted her head upward toward Joe. "I'm really thirsty."

Joe brought her a tall glass of water. "Okay, just sit there till the cops come. I'm going down to meet them, and I'll take the dog with me." Joe clutched the dog's collar to lead him, although he appeared to be docile enough to just follow. Joe glanced back at Rachel as he passed through the door. Her head was leaning back against the wall and her face was blank with shock.

Within minutes, everyone in the building heard the sirens scream as the police cars and ambulance arrived. It wasn't long before a string of burly cops, clad in green uniforms, raced into the unit. Two glanced at Rachel as they rushed by, while four others pushed ahead. Rachel was still glued to the chair out of sheer horror over what she had seen.

Two other large men walked into the condo. The first was a handsome young man. He stood under the archway to the kitchen, his head just under the top, looking at Rachel. The second man continued to where the other men were standing around the body.

"I'm Detective France," he stated to Rachel, while even more men in green uniforms filed behind him into the living room. His dark hair and jet-black eyebrows framed beautiful blue eyes. "We will need to get a statement from you."

"I remember you," Rachel said, pointing a finger at him. "I met you a few times. You were dating my friend, Nightingale, at the time. Before I moved here."

He smiled at the mention of the name. "Yes, you look familiar to me, too. Rachel, is it?"

"Rachel Barnes."

"Nightingale is now my wife."

"That's wonderful," she said, and then began to babble.

"I had a dream. I didn't know it was Eneida I saw. But I remember the blood on the wall, just like it looks now," she blathered, waving her hand backward, without looking, in the general direction of the blood in the living room. She closed her eyes, relaxed a bit. "I have these dreams. Sometimes. Not often. But they come true."

The detective didn't seem to find her comments to be out of line. Rachel figured he probably was used to people making unusual statements, so this wasn't something he'd never heard before.

"I saw the blood and a body, then everything went dark. I couldn't see who...The next night, tonight, Eneida came to me and said goodbye. I woke Joe -- my husband -- and we got the keys from the office -- I manage the condo." Rachel let her head drop forward so she didn't have to look at the detective.

"Okay," he said. "I'll be right back."

France walked over to the other officers. One had begun taking pictures of the body inside the crate.

"She's gone," another said, standing up from the body after checking her pulse. "Rig has set in."

The detective observed that Eneida's body had been scrunched into the crate, assuming a stiff fetal position, with the arms twisting into an unnatural display around her head. Her throat had been sliced, the officers relayed to him, which explained the blood spray on the wall from the lacerated artery. Consequently, her clothes were stained heavily, and her dark curls were crusted with dried blood. France returned to Rachel.

"You found her in the crate?"

"Yes. I opened it because I thought the dog was inside and he needed to go outside," she said. "Eneida's leg and foot sprang out, all bloody. It was gross."

"I'm sure it was," France said as Joe reentered the unit with the dog. "And you're Joe? You let us in downstairs."

"Yes, sir, Joe Barnes." He reached out his hand to the officer. "This is Eneida's dog – the deceased person over there," he said, nodding in the body's direction. "I took him outside to do his business. No telling how long he's been in here."

"I understand. Smells like a while," France said. "We'll have to take him and all the other animals as evidence."

"Oh, no, you can't take Eneida's animals!" Rachel cried out immediately. "She would be devastated to think her animals went to the pound!"

"I'm sorry, but we have to take them. Once the lab has checked them for any potential evidence, they'll go to the Humane Society. You can collect them from there," the detective said.

"Oh, no-o-o," Rachel wined, shaking her head. "This just keeps getting more awful. Awfuller. Is that a word?"

Joe looked at his wife, who was obviously reeling from the events. "Not sure, Honey. Don't worry about it. We'll claim the animals when they're released, okay?"

"Okay," she said, nodding her head. Whatever Joe said was fine.

"Excuse, me folks," Detective France said as he stepped away with his phone.

The couple watched as more people in different uniforms entered, carrying a stretcher. They continued over to where the body was located. All the uniformed people were tall and large. Burly was an apt description of the men for sure. Even the women were tall and large. Rachel thought all of them looked like they lifted weights and were double dosing on steroids. Being on the short side, she suddenly felt like she had been transported to the world of giants.

When the detective returned, he had instructions for the couple.

"I have called for a matron and she'll be here momentarily," he said. "You two will have to go to your condo and give her the clothes you're wearing."

Rachel looked alarmed. "Why? Are we suspects?"

"No, but your clothes are evidence," he said. "Both of you walked around the crime scene, so you may have picked up valuable evidence that will help us catch the person who did this."

Rachel's eyes traveled to her husband.

"Not a problem," Joe said. "We're happy to do anything that will help."

"Murphy!" Detective France called over to the uniformed officers and then turned back. "Corporal Murphy will accompany you to your condo."

Corporal Murphy walked over from the group assembled around the cages. He was a tall, redheaded, freckle-faced young man. And cute, Rachel couldn't help but think, despite the circumstances.

"Take them to their condo unit. Peggy is on her way to collect the clothes," the detective said.

"Yes, sir," he answered. "Come on, folks. What's the number of your condo?"

"Four thirty-four," Joe said.

"I'll come to your office later after you open," France said to Rachel. "We're going to be here a while. No one will be able to have access to this place until the crime scene unit clears it and the Hazmat team comes in to clean."

"Understood," Joe said. "Come on, Rachel, let's go home."

Rachel followed Joe, looking sadly back at the dog. "Soon, baby," she whispered.

They rode down the elevator in silence with the deputy.

It wasn't long after entering their unit that a chunky woman carrying paper bags appeared. She wore a green uniform like all the others.

"I'm Margaret Scott. You can call me Peggy," she said. With her brown hair tightly pulled back into a ponytail and sans make up, she gave the appearance of what one might envision a prison guard looked like.

Rachel didn't think the name of Peggy suited her. She looked more like an Arnold, as in Schwarzenegger. The biceps on the woman jumped out from under her quarter length sleeves, and she had a set of shoulders to match.

"You," Peggy said, pointing at Joe, "go with Murphy. I'll take this one. You're both going to have to strip and give us your clothes."

Rachel immediately felt her heart jump into her throat.

Joe led Murphy into the bedroom after Peggy handed the officer some paper bags.

"Where do you want to do this?" Peggy asked, looking at Rachel as she stood uneasily in the kitchen.

"Uh, do I have to?"

"Yes, you do."

"The bathroom?"

"That's fine with me," she answered. "Long as it's big enough for both of us."

"It's over here," Rachel said, walking around the corner toward the bathroom.

Once standing inside, Rachel felt like slamming the door. Why couldn't she just take off her clothes and hand them out to the officer? Rachel wondered if the officer was going to watch her undress. Surely, she would turn her back? But, no, that wasn't the case. Officer Scott stood firmly in front of Rachel, hands resting on broad hips, waiting for Rachel to make the first move.

Slowly, Rachel gathered up her housedress into her hands and pulled it over her head. Underneath she had on a nightie. "Do you need this, too?"

"I don't think that will be necessary," Officer Scott said. "I'll need your shoes, though."

Rachel handed over the housedress. The cop loosely let it fall into one of the paper bags. Rachel slipped her feet from the flipflops, bent over to pick them up, and then held them out to the larger woman.

"Here you go, Peggy," Rachel said, dropping her shoes into the bag.

To Rachel's horror, Scott took out a small camera and told her to stand with her hands to her sides. She did as told, while the woman photographed her, front and back, head to toe, palms up, palms down, and everything in between, until all of Rachel's body was recorded for evidence. She felt violated from the experience.

"You'll be notified if you can pick up your clothes—or not," the officer said as she turned to open the door. Rachel quickly grabbed a bathrobe from the hook attached and threw it on. It happened to be one of Joe's, so the gray terry robe hung to the floor.

When they walked out, Joe and Murphy had already finished with the undressing. Her husband was standing barefoot in the middle of the living room wearing one of her bathrobes, the pink one. Her favorite one with ruffles and lace. She thought he looked really silly dressed in her robe, with the hem barely reaching his knobby knees. Rachel shook her head at the sight.

"You couldn't find a better bathrobe?" she asked.

"You're wearing mine!" he said. "I wasn't prepared to need a bathrobe on demand."

"Okay, folks," Corporal Murphy said, "we'll leave you now so you can get some sleep."

Joe and Rachel looked at the officer like his hair had morphed from red to black.

What sleep?

EIGHT

AFTER BEING AWAKENED by police sirens, followed by the ambulance, the entire condo was buzzing the next day about the early morning disturbance. It didn't take much to get the residents stirred up, but with something meaty to chew on, all bedlam broke out. Anyone who was mobile came into the office for details. Those who weren't capable of making a personal appearance called on the phone. It was a morning straight from hell for Rachel. And she wasn't in the best of shape to handle the onslaught.

Rachel had a raging headache. She fumbled around in her desk drawer and tried to locate some Ibuprofen. She really needed something today. Whether this would do the trick, she didn't know. When she looked up, Penelope was coming in the door. Rachel just stared into her eyes.

"Lord, child, you don't look too good."

"I'm not good. I found her body." With that statement out of her mouth, she plopped down in the chair.

"I know. I peeked out the door after I heard the sirens. It wasn't hard to figure what happened." Penelope slowly lowered her body to another chair.

"The police will probably want to talk to you," Rachel said, reaching for the mini fridge behind to get bottled water.

"They already have. I gave them my statement."

Rachel's eyes looked over at her hopefully. "Did you hear or see anything?" she asked after she swallowed the pill. Once she started to drink, her thirst took over, and she finished half the bottle.

"No, nothing. I was sound asleep until the sirens went off. Even I can hear sirens. Who do you think murdered her?" The woman's eyes were liquid and full of questions. "It's a scary thought that one of my neighbors has been murdered."

"Yes, it is. For all of us. And I can't imagine who would have killed her, to answer your question." Rachel was still processing the situation, making an effort to be cordial to all the tenants. She understood they were alarmed.

The office door swung open and Detective France entered. He nodded to the women before he spoke.

"I'd like a word with you, Mrs. Barnes."

"Oh, I'll leave you alone now," Penelope said quickly, realizing she needed to leave. She popped from the chair and scooted out the door. Rachel knew that the old woman was tempted to place her ear on the door from the other side. *Hopefully, she'll think better of that and go back to her apartment.*

"Have a seat," Rachel offered. "Would you like some water or coffee?"

"Water would be nice," he said, taking a seat across the desk from Rachel.

"It's the least I can do." Rachel handed the detective a bottle of water from the fridge. "So, what's happening?"

"The medical examiner has ruled the woman's death as a homicide. Her throat was cut after she suffered a beating. It was brutal," he said, taking a few swallows of water. "The assailant used an object to knock her around before killing her. We speculate that was to weaken her. We did not find that object at the scene. The time of death was probably less than twenty-four hours prior to the discovery of the body."

"Do you have any idea who could have done such a horrific thing?" Rachel needed to know if the other residents were in jeopardy.

"Not yet. Let me ask you something," he said, leaning forward in the chair. "Did this woman routinely cage her cats, if you know?"

"I don't know for sure, but I assume she let them run loose. She was an animal lover, so I don't think she'd want her cats confined. What would be the purpose in that?" Rachel said. "I also used to receive complaints about noise caused by the cats, so I doubt they were caged."

"Was she seeing anyone?"

"Not that I know of. And I'm sure I would have known about that." They were close friends. She would have known. At least that was her thought. "I'm going down to the precinct today to give a complete statement. Joe, too."

"Did she have enemies?"

"Some people in other shelters, like kill shelters, may not have liked her activism, but I'm not aware she had enemies." Who could hate Eneida enough to kill her? That was an impossibility to Rachel.

"What kind of activism?"

"She worked to get all shelters to become no-kill, like hers. You see, it can be more profitable to be a kill shelter, but it's not humane. Eneida was all for the kind treatment of animals."

"I see." The detective sat back in the chair and paused in thought, his eyes running up to the ceiling. "Was she anxious about anything happening in her life?"

"Actually, things were going very well for her. She had hired a man to run the shelter about a year ago, so she had more free time. I can't imagine anyone with any significant reason for killing her," Rachel said, looking wide eyed at the detective. "She was a good person, a friend."

"Please write down that person's name and contact information, the man at the shelter," the detective said, standing. "And the shelter name and address."

"Certainly."

"I'll let you know as much as I'm allowed as the case progresses. I can't be specific about an on-going case. If you think of anything that might be helpful, give me a call."

"I will," she said, writing Jorge's name and information on a piece of notepaper and sliding it across the desk to him. "When can we claim the animals?"

"Soon. Maybe in two days, I would think."

"Good."

The detective left her office, leaving Rachel to puzzle over last night's events.

NINE

AT THE POINT Rachel thought everyone had made their entrance and exit, in walked Loretta. She was dressed impeccably in her usual attire of a pantsuit, this one lemon yellow, even though the temperature was well into the nineties.

"Rachel, dear, you look tired," Loretta said as she sat across from Rachel

"I didn't get a lot of sleep last night." That was certainly an honest statement.

"I can understand that." Loretta looked compassionately at Rachel. "Eneida was your friend, wasn't she?"

"Yes. So, I'm more than a little upset by all of this." Rachel sank back into her chair. "I can't imagine who would want her dead."

"There are a lot of sickos roaming around. I've had encounters with more than my share of degenerates. A police detective rarely associates with wholesome people when on the job."

"I can imagine. You should write a book."

"I did, but none of the publishers would accept it because they recognized some of the characters, despite the name changes,"

Loretta said, folding her hands in her lap. "Apparently, news of my investigations traveled a wide circuit."

"So, now you're here, retired and enjoying life," Rachel said.

"Yes. But this murder in our building has me disturbed," Loretta said. "I just wonder if there could be another attempt on someone's life."

"Are you afraid someone from your past came looking for you?" That thought had not entered Rachel's mind until now. All she needed was to have a once high-profile detective murdered in the condo. The headlines would be sensational.

"I rubbed elbows undercover with some very, shall we say, influential men. And many went to prison because of me. Anything is possible," Loretta said, looking down at her manicured hands. "It's difficult to know who might want to seek revenge after they get out of prison."

"Loretta, we have a secure building. I really believe this is an isolated situation having nothing to do with you." Rachel sat up closer to her desk. "I don't see any connection with the murder of an animal shelter owner and a former detective. It is highly unlikely whoever committed this murder will return. I think you are safe here."

"If it's so safe here, how did a murderer gain entry?" The words came out quickly.

"You have a very good point. I don't have an answer for that at this time." Rachel was not feeling well and these questions for which she did not have answers were making her uncomfortable and a bit insecure. "We'll have to see what the police determine happened."

"You're right. There's no sense in worrying about something that we haven't any control over and could very well be random," Loretta said, standing to leave. "I just thought I'd come by to see what you knew."

"Not much right now. I'm sorry."

"Good bye, dear," she said as she closed the door behind her.

Finally alone, Rachel put her arms on the desk, lowered her head, and sobbed.

. . .

"Yes, I know you miss her," Rachel said as she knelt in front of the dog. The confiscated animals had been released from evidence, as promised, and sent to the Humane Society. Joe picked up the dog and brought him home to Rachel. Then Jorge and Joe also claimed the cats and brought them back to Eneida's shelter.

She fondled the dog's ears and looked into his moist brown eyes, as if seeking a clue how to console him. "What was your name?" She had a lapse of memory about what Eneida called him.

Rachel fumbled around with his collar for his identification, finally reading the name on the tag. "Ah, Rufus! Yes, that totally suits you, big boy. *Rufus...*" she said, anchoring the name into her mind. "Well, you're here with us now, so you'll have to get used to it. And get to know Joe. I predict, you will love him. And he'll love you, too."

Right on cue, Joe walked in the front door of their apartment, carrying a bag of groceries. Rufus leaped at Joe, his big hairy paws resting on the man's chest, all but dislodging the bag. Rufus' tongue hung sideways as he appeared to smile at his new daddy.

"He likes you," Rachel said.

"Yeah, I see that. Dog has good taste." Joe nudged at Rufus.

"You need to train him not to jump on you," Rachel said. "For all her good qualities, Eneida was not much in the training department. He shouldn't jump on people. Especially being so large."

"Yeah, he's not a pipsqueak dog." Joe broke the hold Rufus had on him. "Down...What's his name?"

"Rufus."

"Oh, I like that. Rufus." Joe patted the animal on the head. "Good Rufus."

"Good Rufus needs dog food."

"Yeah, I got some. I left it in the walkway. Let me put down this bag on the counter and I'll get it." Joe walked outside where an open walkway fronted all the units on each floor, stretching the length of the building.

"Good Joe." Rachel grinned.

TEN

RUFUS SAT QUIETLY, eyeballing every bite of toast Joe put into his mouth. The dog licked his lips when a blob of scrambled egg followed, his eyes fixated on the man.

"This is mine," Joe said to the dog. "All mine."

Rufus thumped his tail on the floor, his face saying, "Mine, too."

"Oh, brother, look at you two," Rachel said as she walked by them and into the kitchen. "Don't turn your back or Rufus will swallow up your breakfast in one sweep of that tongue."

"I have no intention of taking my eyes off this plate," Joe said, taking a generous portion of egg onto his fork. "What are you doing up so early?"

"I can't sleep. I just keep seeing the blood on the wall and then I feel miserable," she said, pulling the carafe from the coffee maker and pouring a cup of coffee. "And Eneida came into my dreams last night."

"Again? What happened?"

"She looked scared this time, like she was puzzled by what happened. I need to say prayers for her." Rachel gave her husband a wide-eyed look.

"That is a very good idea." Joe shoved the last bite of toast into his mouth and placed the empty plate on the tile floor. Rufus slurped down any meager remnants of egg and crumbs. "Was she religious?"

"Well, she seemed spiritual. As for religious, I'm not sure. She was Catholic when she was younger." Rachel sat across from her husband, coffee cup in hand.

"Then you need to say some prayers for sure, and I will, too," Joe said. Oddly, Joe was the more religious one.

"I will."

"And now she's continuing to visit you in your sleep?" Joe gathered his keys and wallet as he spoke.

"Yes. That's why I think she needs our prayers."

"Hear that, Rufus? Mama's being visited by your first mama." Joe patted the dog when he raised his head from incessantly cleaning the plate.

"You really shouldn't let him lick the plate, Joe."

"What's the difference? It's going into the dishwasher, isn't it?"

"Yes, but...never mind." She was too tired to discuss it.

"Okay, I'm out of here," Joe said, walking toward the door. "I'll be upstairs trying to see what's happening with the clean up after that fight the Rogers had. Then I'll see if there's any action at Eneida's place."

"Bye." Rachel remained seated in her chair, slightly numb over her present life.

Joe had just exited the elevator when he heard a loud slam. Looking down the open-air walkway, he saw Marc Rogers furiously slamming his condo door, over and over. "What the heck are you doing?" Joe asked as he walked closer to the man.

"Door won't stay shut!" Marc kept closing the door until Joe reached him.

"Knock it off! You've probably sprung it by slamming it like that." Joe inserted himself between Marc and the door. "Step away."

Marc did as he was told, stepping back about three feet from Joe and the door. He positioned himself against the railing that safely prevented him from falling several flights downward.

"Yeah, you've busted the door," Joe said while examining the damage. "I'll have to fix it or it won't lock."

"Don't bother," Marc said. "I don't care if it locks or not."

Joe turned toward Marc, noticing his appearance wasn't suitable for public viewing. His hair was messy and he had on a ratty tee-shirt over his blue cutoff jeans. One of his arms had a sleeve of tattoos, the other only one heart. The sleeved arm appeared to be mostly biker related in theme, fitting a man who owned a bike shop. His feet were bare.

"Well, your wife just might like to feel safe by being able to lock the door," Joe said. "You two have another fight?"

"Yeah. So what? You and your wife never fight?" The expression he wore was full of rage and he appeared nervous as he wiped the back of his hand across his bleeding nose.

"Not like that."

Marc didn't have a reply.

"I'm going to get my tools. Is Lola okay?"

"Yeah, why wouldn't she be?" Marc was getting testier the longer they talked.

"Oh, I don't know, by the looks of you I'd guess she took a swing after you hit her."

"She's a crazy woman," Marc said, turning away to spit blood over the railing of the walkway. "I think I'm losing a tooth because of her."

"Well, don't spit it down there on someone," Joe said. "I'll be back shortly."

On his way to the maintenance closet, Joe had to walk by Eneida's unit. Yellow crime scene tape was stretched across the doorway. No detectives seemed to be around at the time. He was curious about the investigation, such as, if they had any leads yet?

Joe arrived at his maintenance closet and unlocked the deadbolt. As his hand reached out to turn the doorknob, he caught a glimpse out of the corner of his eye of a person approaching. It was Ruby, all decked out in an aggressively red bathing suit that almost matched the color of her hair.

"Hello, Joe," Ruby said, giving him a bright smile. "I see Rachel has you working hard."

"You could say that, Ruby."

"Why don't you come to my place for a cup of tea?" Ruby suggested, replacing the fallen strap on her bony shoulder.

The woman doesn't have enough meat on her bones to keep her clothes in place, Joe thought.

"I can't. I've got to tend to a broken door," Joe said. "But thanks for the invite."

Ruby smiled brightly again. "Any time, Joe."

Joe liked Ruby. She was certainly a character, but he appreciated that quality. He watched her sashay her hips as she walked away. All ninety pounds of her. He couldn't help but notice that she didn't have a fanny anymore. He shook his head.

Joe returned to the Rogers apartment to repair the damaged door, knocking loudly so the occupants knew he was there.

"I'm repairing your door, just so you know," Joe called out as he pushed open the door. "Holy cow."

What he saw was an apartment that looked like one of the hurricanes from last year had made a repeat appearance. Lamps were on their sides, furniture turned wrong, pictures torn off the walls and tossed, and broken glass collected in various areas of the floor. The apartment smelled like everything Lola had cooked over the last few days. Most of that was on the floor, too. Were they throwing food at each other?

"Rachel won't like this," Joe muttered to himself.

After he'd been working on the repairs for a while, Lola crept from the bedroom. She was presentably dressed in shorts and a top, but one eye was blackened and her lips looked swollen.

Oh, there certainly had been a fight.

"Hello, Lola," Joe said, glancing in her direction as she drew closer. "Had another fight, huh?"

"Nothing bad, just a little one," she replied sheepishly.

"Yeah? I'd hate to see the end result of a bad one," he remarked, nodding his head toward the living room. "When are you planning to clean up that mess? Or is some of it left from the last fight?"

"Maybe."

Joe stopped what he was doing and turned to look more closely at Lola. Minus her bruises, Lola would have been an attractive woman. She had a rather muscular body, indicating she had participated in sports at some point in her life. He knew her to use the tennis court regularly. Obviously, she was quite capable of landing punches to Marc's face.

"Why do you put up with this, Lola? Why don't you leave Marc?" Joe was genuinely concerned about the abuse, remembering back to his own childhood. That was not a good memory.

"Leave? I wouldn't leave Marc." Her eyes grew big and she squared her shoulders with indignation. "He's my husband and I love him."

Joe swung his arm toward the room. "This doesn't look like love. This looks like abuse."

"Marc loves me. He just has a bad temper."

"Oh, I can see he has a temper, all right. No question there." Joe focused on the door again.

"When he comes home, he'll help me clean up." She smiled and giggled a little. "He'll probably bring me roses, too."

"Yeah, roses for your funeral's more like it." Joe shook his head in disgust, turning back to face her.

Lola dropped her head and looked away. "Marc loves me," she said, her voice barely audible When she turned her head back, Joe could see tears in her eyes.

"Lola, you don't have to put up with his abuse," Joe said, stepping away from the door and closer to her. "There are shelters you can go to for protection."

With her eyes welling to capacity, Lola reached out to Joe, throwing her arms around him. The distraught woman clung to him, sobbing into his chest. Joe froze in position, his body becoming as wooden as a toy soldier.

"Now, Lola, it's okay," he said, awkwardly patting her on the back with one hand while trying to disengage himself from her embrace with the other. "Here, stand up straight, wipe your eyes. It's okay."

"No, it's not." Lola's mouth opened wide as she released a pitiful wailing sound.

"Do you want me to call Rachel? I can get her here in a minute," he suggested. This was more than Joe could handle. And it was awkward.

"No-o-o-o," Lola moaned, her face all scrunched up in the ugly cry. She turned toward the bedroom and skipped inside, closing the door behind her.

"Wait till Rachel hears about this," Joe muttered to himself.

He made quick work repairing the door and left before Lola decided to come out of the bedroom again.

ELEVEN

RUFUS WAS LICKING Rachel's knee when Joe entered her office. Immediately, the dog ceased and sprang at Joe.

"Down, Rufus!" Joe removed the dog's paws from his chest and let him drop to the floor. "Good boy. Down is good."

"It's going to take time to break him of that habit," Rachel said.

"I see that."

"Any signs of cleanup at the Rogers' apartment?"

"Not really. I just finished repairing the front door."

Rachel turned away from the desk, focusing fully on Joe. "What was wrong with the door?"

"Marc broke it slamming it shut a dozen times, is my guess. I caught him and stopped him from doing more damage," Joe said, easing into a chair across the desk from Rachel.

Rachel looked questioningly at him. "That doesn't make sense." She had chosen the turquoise blouse she was wearing because it made her blue eyes stand out. Rachel knew her husband liked it when she wore blue. She was sure he noticed.

"It does if you saw the apartment. They had a fight and the place is trashed again. Or maybe still. I bet it never got cleaned up after their last one." He shrugged.

"I can't allow this to continue. That man is going to kill her if something isn't done."

"Well, don't look at Lola to do anything. She's sporting a fresh black eye and swollen lips." He pointed at the mini fridge to indicate he wanted a bottle of water. "Marc had a bloody nose. She must have clocked him because he was spitting blood. Said he was losing a tooth."

"This situation is totally out of hand. She needs to leave that jerk and go to a shelter," Rachel said, handing a bottle of water to Joe and opening one for herself.

"Yeah, well, that was my suggestion to her and she just says she loves him. She isn't going anywhere." Joe took a long drink from the bottle.

"I need to inform the Morgans about their tenants. They probably have no clue what's going on there."

"Whatever you think best."

"And you said the place is trashed — again?"

"Or additionally. Hard to tell, but it's a mess."

Rachel reached for her telephone log. "I'm calling the Morgans. I've had enough. They need to evict their tenants."

"I also went by Eneida's apartment and there isn't any action there. No cops in sight."

"Detective France will let me know if something's happening." Rachel looked over at her husband. He was her support system, always calm and steady when she was on the brink of an emotional drop. "Poor Eneida."

"Is there going to be a funeral?" Olivia asked as she dabbed a tissue carefully at her eyes so as not to smear her mascara.

"As far as I know, yes. I haven't spoken directly with her oldest daughter, but Detective France indicated the family was taking care of things," Rachel said, taking another sip of her iced tea and reaching for a complimentary cookie. "Her kids are scattered around and her ex-husband is deceased. The only child in Florida is Margarita, but she's in Miami. It's difficult for her to arrange something from down there."

"I just can't understand who would kill her," Tia said, the casual yellow top she wore accentuating her dark complexion and black hair. "She was a good person, loved animals. Why do this to her?"

"I haven't an answer. All I know is, there are sickos out there who like to harm people," Rachel said. "These last few days for me have been straight from hell. And I am absolutely exhausted."

Olivia lifted her glass and smiled at the server the next time she looked over from the bar. "Well, you found her body. I can understand that would be upsetting."

"Upsetting? There was blood on the wall. It fanned out and dripped down. The bastard slit her throat!" Rachel said. "Blood was everywhere. That was the grossest thing I've ever seen. Of course, I'm upset." Rachel's face matched the red color in her patterned blouse.

Olivia and Tia exchanged looks of concern. In an attempt to lead the conversation elsewhere, Tia said, "What about the shelter? Eneida owned the shelter. What will happen to that?"

"I don't know. She probably had a will and made provisions, I would think," Rachel said. "The shelter was too important to her not to have made some sort of arrangement."

Olivia accepted her fresh iced tea from the server, took a sip and set the glass down. "What do you know about the man who manages the shelter?"

"Let's see, his name is Jorge Benitez. He's in his late forties, I think. Seems nice enough," Rachel said, reaching into her purse and rummaging around for her fan. "He takes very good care of the shelter. Eneida thought he was great or she wouldn't have trusted him with the animals."

"He has to be a nice man," Olivia agreed. "He's probably upset by this situation."

A shadow fell over the table as a man drew close. The three women looked up to see Alfred.

"Hello, ladies," he said in a soft breathy voice.

"Hello, Alfred. How are you this fine evening?" Rachel asked, fanning herself.

"Rosy, just peachy." The old guy fumbled in his pockets as if he were looking for something. "You ladies look like you're having a good time."

"Yes, we are," Olivia said.

Alfred looked from one face to the other. It wasn't clear what he wanted. Maybe he expected to be invited to join them?

"Awful, just awful about that woman being murdered," Alfred finally said. "I hope we don't have a serial killer on the premises."

"I wouldn't worry about that, Alfred," Rachel said. "There hasn't been any indication in that direction. I'm quite sure you're safe in your unit."

Alfred made a nervous giggling response. "Well, if you say so, I believe you."

"Everything will be fine, Alfred," Tia assured him.

"Okay, ladies, have a nice evening." Alfred shuffled away from the table, seemingly satisfied he wasn't in harm's way.

"Bye, Alfred," each called after him.

"Okay, I'm going to the lady's room," Olivia said, rising from her chair. Rachel and Tia chuckled as she headed toward the restrooms, trying her best to look like a lady.

"I wonder how Olivia's date went," Tia said.

"Let's ask her when she gets back." Rachel sipped her tea, quietly sitting in her chair. "I really like these little soirees we have. It helps me unwind being with you two." *Used to be three*, Rachel thought.

Olivia returned to the table.

Rachel locked her eyes on Olivia. "Okay, we both want to know how your date went."

"It was nice." Olivia adjusted herself back into her chair.

"Huh uh, more, give us more," Rachel said. "You can't just say that it was nice."

"Well, he was a gentleman..."

"*Bo-ring*," Rachel said.

"He was not boring. He was respectful." Olivia's lips curved into a slight smile. "Nice looking, too, just like his picture. He seemed to like me and I liked him."

"Are you going out again?" Tia asked.

"Yes."

"When?" Rachel asked.

"When he gets back from his trip."

"A likely story," Rachel said, giving her fan a hearty flip in the air.

"No, really. He has a medical conference in Sacramento. He'll be gone a week." Olivia kept smiling, her pleasure obvious. "When he returns, my doctor friend will call me and we'll go out to dinner again. Italian this time. He likes Italian food."

Rachel's eyes crinkled as she smiled at her friend. "I hope it works out for you. I really do."

"We'll just have to wait and see," Olivia said, grinning, and then looking down into her lap as her cheeks flushed.

"A toast to a budding relationship!" Tia said, hoisting her glass.

"*Cheers!*"

Rachel walked into the apartment, feeling a little sad and sporting what felt like a strong buzz. She tried to be quiet because, even though she had gotten home early, Joe was sure to be in bed. She carefully negotiated over the rug that had been her undoing previously, not wanting to fall and wake her husband from a deep sleep again.

But then Rachel hadn't considered Rufus. The dog had other ideas.

A giant yellow blur leaped at her in his eagerness to greet Rachel. Wham, she was thrown right to the floor with a loud thud, followed by some moaning. Slobbery kisses were delivered to any exposed skin, especially her face, as Rufus straddled Rachel's body.

"Phffffttt, leave me alone, Rufus!" she hollered, trying unsuccessfully to push the dog away. "I can't breathe! Get your tongue out of my nose!"

Rachel could hear Joe stomping across the floor to rescue her.

"I'll get him," Joe said, pulling Rufus back by his collar.

"Ugh, I'm all wet!" Rachel rolled over and got up. "Oh, you hairy, slobbery beast!" She glared at Rufus who just sat wagging his tail as he looked adoringly at her.

"So, did you have fun tonight?" Joe asked.

"If you call fun talking about Eneida's death and being attacked by Sasquatch."

He grinned. "Okay, Rufus, I guess you're the one who had all the fun tonight. Let's go back to bed." Joe led the dog away. "Mamma needs to clean up." Rachel was sure she heard him chuckle after that last remark.

After a shower, Rachel climbed in bed, ready for a good night's sleep. But that wasn't happening. She threw off the covers, hoping the ceiling fan would cool her off. But that made her cold, so she pulled the covers up again. After a few minutes, Rachel was sweating. Finally, she did a half up and down position with the covers, slinging one leg and one arm totally outside, hoping that would be comfortable for her body. And it was for a while, then she got cold again. Ah, one of *those* nights...Eventually, sleep took her.

TWELVE

FIVE DAYS FOLLOWING Eneida's death, Detective France entered Rachel's office, surprising her.

Rachel stood to greet him from behind her desk. "Hello, Detective. Come in and have a seat." She probably looked to the detective like she was going to a funeral because she was all in black.

"Thank you." He sat in the chair, looking like he had news to tell. "I thought you'd want to know that Eneida's daughter is taking charge of the body and preparing for her to be cremated."

"Really?"

"I believe it had to do with finances. And Eneida's will."

"Oh, so she did have a will...I thought she would have one," Rachel said, nodding. "She would want the shelter taken care of after her death."

"Yes, apparently all the money she left in her will and life insurance is to go to the shelter. Some money was set aside for Eneida's burial but, given the expense, the daughter thought cremation was best," France said.

"I see."

"The daughter has your contact information. I thought you'd want her to have it since you were close to her mother."

"Yes, thank you. All I ever knew was that her name was Margarita and she lived in Miami. I never met her," Rachel said. "I definitely want to be at any memorial she has planned."

"She didn't say anything about that, but here's Margarita's phone number if you want to call her," France said, handing Rachel a sheet of paper. "And thanks to you and Joe for giving your statement. You do understand that we had to fingerprint you for elimination purposes?"

"That's okay. We do understand. Thank you for Margarita's number. I certainly will call her." Rachel placed the paper in the top drawer of her desk. "Any news about the investigation?"

"Not too much. We figure she knew her assailant and let the person enter the building because there was no forced entry into her apartment. The only fingerprints we found were hers and yours. And some smudged ones on the latch, which were probably yours. We surmise whoever came to visit was a friend, because we found two wine glasses, but we couldn't get any DNA to confirm an identity since the glasses were smashed and contaminated by the animals."

"Hmm, so she knew the person..." Rachel found that interesting.

"Do you know anyone who would have visited her apartment? Besides you."

"No, not really. And I hadn't been up there in a couple months myself." Rachel looked a little guiltily at the detective. "Since I'm the manager, sometimes I avoid things. Eneida kept animals up there and I sort of ignored how many or if she was in violation of the rules. She was a friend and I didn't want to have to take issue with her."

"I understand. Is there anyone in the building she was friendly with?"

"Besides me, there were two friends, Olivia Johnson and Tia Patel. But neither of them murdered her. Olivia is a professor and Tia's a doctor." Rachel reached behind to her mini fridge, opened the door and withdrew a bottle of water. "Would you like some water?"

"Yes, please." He accepted the water and twisted off the lid. "Thank you."

"Both women adored Eneida." Rachel pulled out a bottle for herself and was surprised to see that it was the last one. "Otherwise, she knew people on a casual basis who live here in the building. But many of these people are elderly, hardly capable of committing that violent murder scene I saw."

"But *everyone* here isn't elderly, are they?" France raised the bottle of water to his lips.

"No, you just have to be over fifty to live here," Rachel answered.

"Can you think of anyone who is on the younger side that might be capable of violence?"

"Well, yes, I can. Marc Rogers." She didn't hesitate to share information about the noisy, destructive couple. "He owns a bike shop and he abuses his wife on a regular basis. I'm going to get the owners who rent to the couple to evict them."

"I'd like you to delay that for now until this investigation is over. What apartment does he live in?" France pulled out his notepad.

"Eighth floor, apartment 809."

"Right next to the victim's unit? Okay, I'll let you know if I find anything of interest from him that should concern you," he said, rising.

"I appreciate that," Rachel said.

"I'll go upstairs now and see if Marc is home," Detective France said.

"Thank you for the information you shared." Rachel also stood as the detective walked toward the door of her office and out. She buzzed the door for him so he could get into the elevator area. Then she went to her own unit to get more water for her mini-fridge.

Detective France pulled out his ringing cell phone from his pocket while he was on the elevator, heading for the eighth floor. He answered the call with a quick, "Yeah."

"Hi, Honey," a sweet voice said. "I'm planning spaghetti for tonight and maybe something special for dessert."

He chuckled. "Okay, that sounds good. I should be home by six."

"Great! Then I know when to start the meatballs."

"Love you," he said.

"Love you," she said.

He exited the elevator, continued down the walkway, and stood before the door of apartment 809. Before the detective could knock, he heard a woman screaming. Gurgled or muted sounds followed, he wasn't sure which. With his adrenalin surging suddenly, France tried the door. Finding it unlocked, he pushed inside as he yelled, "Police!"

His view was clear, being that the room flowed from the front door directly to the balcony. France saw Marc vigorously choking his wife with his bare hands. She was partially bent backwards over the balcony railing. He hastily moved to the balcony, cautiously trampling over and around debris for the length of the dining and living room, not sure if the man was trying to choke his wife or additionally throw her over the railing.

Lola began to squirm with more strength under Marc's grip. It soon became apparent that Marc had decided to hoist Lola over the railing, because he released the hold on her neck and grabbed the bottom of her shorts with both hands, attempting to lift her. Lola clawed at his face and screamed full force, the sound ripping through the air like a siren.

Now on the balcony, France hooked one arm around Marc's neck, throwing him off balance. He grabbed at Lola's arm, jerking her toward him and then to the side. She fell safely onto the balcony. When Marc regained his posture, he looked confused and didn't resist the detective as he took physical control of the man. France pulled Marc's arms behind his back and handcuffed him.

"Okay, that's the end of your fun. You're going to jail," France said, maneuvering Marc ahead, directing him toward the front door, again trying to avoid debris along the way.

He glanced back at Lola, who was still on the floor of the balcony. As he was about to say something to her, she began to yell at him.

"Oh, no, what's happening?" Lola cried. She rose from the balcony floor and slinked along beside the two men as they made their way to the door. "You can't take him away!"

The detective gave Lola a sideways glance as he continued to muscle the wiry man forward. She began screaming profanities at France and beating him with her fists. Most blows hit his arms, others his back.

"Ma'am, I'm going to have to arrest you if you don't stop," he said.

"You stop! That's my husband!" She continued pummeling the detective.

"Lady, you're insane," France said, pressing the communication button at his collar to notify dispatch as he simultaneously kicked his leg out at Lola. The encounter sent her reeling to the wall. "Stay there! Don't move!"

When dispatch answered, France called for assistance in a domestic abuse situation and clicked off. He looked over at Lola, who was frozen against the wall, sliding downward until she came to rest on her heels.

"Sit," he ordered Marc, shoving him into a ratty beige chair that looked like it had been adorned with blood stains from their past altercations. "Don't move."

France turned to Lola, now cowering on the floor. He pulled out a set of zip ties, reached down for Lola's arm, pulled her up and around, and then clamped the ties on her wrists.

"Satisfied now?" France asked.

Watching his wife being restrained sent Marc into a frenzy. Springing from the chair, he kicked at France's back. The detective whirled around and the two men fell to the floor, tussling on the carpet among the broken glass and food. All through the altercation, Lola screamed bloody murder. If he hadn't already called for backup, the neighbors surely would have called the police.

France was finally able to contain Marc's wriggling around by sitting on his chest. He looked over at Lola who was standing at attention with her back against the wall. He only waited a few seconds more before reinforcements barged through the door. Six beefy men and one formidable woman entered, quickly gathering around France and Marc.

"Place these two under arrest." Standing up from Marc's body, he pointed at Marc. "Him, attempted murder, domestic abuse, and assault on a police officer." Jerking his thumb towards Lola, he continued. "Her, assault on an officer."

France strode from the apartment, adjusting his shoulders as he waited for the elevator. It was then he realized he had picked up the stench of the Rogers' apartment on himself. Two more officers exited with the EMTs. His plan was to make short work with the report and head home for a shower, a spaghetti dinner.

And dessert.

THIRTEEN

PENELOPE WAS the first one to enter Rachel's office the next morning, barely giving her time to get seated.

"I saw the cops taking Marc out in handcuffs, and Lola, too. What happened?"

Rachel debated how much she wanted to tell the woman. She didn't need the entire complex gossiping about Marc and Lola.

"It's hard to say right now. I don't have all the facts." Rachel hoped that would satisfy the woman.

"I heard Lola yelling like someone was cutting off her fingers and toes," Penelope said. "It was awful. Do you think Marc was chopping off her digits?"

"I seriously doubt that. I received several calls about the noise," Rachel said, pushing the button on the coffeemaker sitting atop the mini fridge. She really needed some caffeine.

"It was more than noise. Lola was screaming at the top of her lungs. You know how kids shriek when playing? It was like that. Shrill. Ear splitting. I know Marc was trying to kill her," Penelope said with assurance.

"We'll let the police determine that. Let's not start something going around that we aren't sure about." Rachel raised her eyebrows to indicate she meant business.

"Oh, of course. I saw Marc on the balcony," Penelope said, deciding to sit down to continue her tale. "He was choking Lola before that detective fella arrived. I know Marc was all set to heave Lola over until the detective disturbed his plan."

Rachel turned her eyes on Penelope in disbelief over what she was hearing. *What was wrong with that man?*

"If the detective hadn't come along, she'd be splattered like a cantaloupe all over the sidewalk below," Penelope said. "He cuffed Marc, just like on TV. I saw it all from my balcony."

Rachel was sure Penelope had viewed the whole scene with glee, since she lived next door to the feuding couple and took pleasure in reporting on the Rogers' activities. Having seen the actual cuffing of Marc, unfortunately, would only add to her gossip.

"Lola was caterwauling the whole time. I could hear her through the walls. But I was surprised when she was taken from the apartment in zip ties. I peeked out my peephole in the door," she admitted somewhat giddily. "What do you suppose caused that?" Penelope was sitting on the edge of her chair, intently looking at Rachel for answers.

"I don't know, dear." She wasn't going to admit that France had told her about the entire fight.

"I'll bet he killed Eneida. He's a violent man, that Marc," Penelope said with an affirmative nod. She tightened her sweater around her chest.

"Oh, please, don't go around telling anyone that you suspect he killed Eneida," Rachel said. "We have no proof of that."

"I won't say a word if you don't want me to," Penelope said. "But I think he did it."

"Thinking and facts can vary greatly. I don't even know of any connection between Eneida and Marc — or Lola, for that matter.

That's just guess work on your part." Rachel looked sternly at the elder woman. "Please, don't say *anything*."

"I promise, Rachel. My lips are sealed." Penelope rose to leave. "But I know he did it."

Rachel rolled her eyes as the woman exited her office, pulling her sweater even tighter around her shoulders.

"Oh, geez..." Rachel murmured to herself. "What a way to start the day. The smell of coffee was tantalizing, and was a true pleasure as she added the necessary three sugars and sipped her first cup, calming her a bit.

She tried to settle into work, but was plagued by the haunting idea of Eneida having been murdered by Marc. *Was that even a possibility?*

"Don't look so serious," came a male voice, interrupting her thoughts.

Rachel looked over to see Joe in the doorway.

"Hey, I have a lot on my mind," she answered.

"And what's happening now? Anymore dead bodies show up?" Joe sat across from Rachel.

"That's really not an appropriate question."

"Okay, so I'm a tacky guy. What's wrong?"

"Penelope was just here. She thinks Marc murdered Eneida." Rachel looked imploringly at her husband. "Is that even possible?"

A wrinkle creased between his eyes before he spoke. "Anything's possible. Sounds kinda crazy to me, but who knows?"

"I don't believe it and I don't want her spreading such a preposterous idea around the complex. We don't need to add any fuel to this situation," Rachel said.

"I agree with that. But it's possible," Joe said. "What connection was there between Marc and Eneida?"

"I don't know of any, Joe. To my knowledge, they were practically strangers."

"Hmm, well, I don't know what to say."

"Is the crime scene tape still on Eneida's door?"

"Yes." Joe adjusted in his seat, trying to get more comfortable in the prissy chair Rachel had selected. It wasn't comfortable. But maybe that was to discourage long visits. "What about the Rogers? Any more news?"

"Lola was bonding out, last I heard. But she doesn't want to press charges against Marc. She claims he wasn't trying to kill her, that they were just having one of their normal fights. Give me a break." Rachel rolled her eyes.

"So, what are they going to charge them with?" Joe asked.

"For Lola, I think it might end up only assault on a police officer. If she won't testify, I don't think the prosecutors will press the issue with Marc. Too many cases on their docket, it seems," Rachel said, shrugging her shoulders. "At least that was what Detective France is speculating will happen."

"So, he gets away with abuse again." Joe rose from the chair. "And maybe he's guilty of Eneida's death as well."

"Stop saying that! We don't know," Rachel said.

"He's a mean guy. So, maybe..."

"We don't know. We have no proof," Rachel insisted.

Joe looked at his wife with eyes that spoke his thoughts. Rachel knew that he believed Marc was guilty. Of something.

The office door swung open. Rachel looked over to see Ruby and Loretta, shoulder to shoulder. Both women, although each as skinny as a mailing tube, could not fit through the door at the same time. One had to let the other go first. Ruby stepped back and pushed Loretta forward.

"Age before beauty," Ruby said with a smirk.

With a backward glance at Ruby, Loretta entered the office. "Good morning, Rachel." She sat in the chair before Ruby could get to it. Ruby stood, glaring at Loretta.

"What can I do for you two ladies this morning?" Rachel really didn't want to hear the reply.

"We're here because we understand that Lola was almost murdered yesterday," Ruby said, all of her bony joints sticking out from her sundress.

"And we're concerned that there's an epidemic of hostility afoot," Loretta said, folding her elegant hands in her lap over her lime green pantsuit. Rachel couldn't help but wonder if she owned a dress.

"What?"

"People are getting murdered here," Ruby said.

"Wait a minute. Only one person has been murdered," Rachel said, immediately recognizing that statement didn't come out right.

"One is enough," Loretta said.

"There's a killer on the loose," Ruby said.

"Lola was not murdered," Rachel said, exasperation creeping into her voice. "*One* murder. We've experienced one murder. And a killer is not running around murdering women at this complex. That's just not true."

"What are you doing about this situation?" Ruby asked.

"Yes, Rachel, what steps have you taken for our security?" Loretta asked, staring directly at Rachel as if fully anticipating a satisfactory answer.

Rachel was amazed that these two women were grilling her. What was even more astounding, they seemed to be united in their confrontation. They didn't even like each other! Ruby, especially, despised Loretta, for reasons still unknown to Rachel.

"I can assure you both that this is a secure building. I believe it is all right for me to say that the person who killed Eneida was probably known to her. It appears she let him or her into her apartment. There is no evidence of a forced entry," Rachel said, reaching to get herself a two liter bottle of water. "It was an isolated incident."

"But someone died," Loretta said.

"I know that. Eneida was my friend," Rachel said, beginning to tear up. "Don't you think I feel badly about this? Has anyone considered my feelings? You two are acting like I was lax in my duties and because of my negligence, someone was murdered. But that just isn't the case."

The two women remained silent for a moment before Ruby spoke.

"I'm sorry, Rachel. I didn't consider your feelings in this situation. You do run a good operation here." Ruby looked down at her sandaled feet. Rachel could see the green toe polish shining.

"People are nervous since the murder and now Lola has suffered an incident, albeit, not a murder. It makes everyone jumpy," Loretta said.

"The feuding between Marc and Lola is well known. Everyone calls me on the phone to report their latest knockdown, drag out affair. Why is anyone surprised they got arrested? If Marc had succeeded in pushing her off the balcony, would anyone have been surprised?" Rachel said, sipping at her coffee, attempting to get in control of her emotions.

"He tried to push her off the balcony?" Ruby said. "Oh, my, that's awful!"

Rachel realized she had let something slip. "Now wait, that isn't information you should spread outside of this room. I shouldn't have said anything, and it really doesn't change the situation you ladies came in here to address," Rachel said. "Please, do not repeat what I said."

"I certainly can be discreet," Loretta said. Rachel believed that Loretta, of all people, being a former detective, knew how to keep her mouth shut.

"Me, too," Ruby said. Rachel doubted Ruby knew how to be discreet. She was the most flamboyant person in the building.

"This is important, ladies. Do not say anything to anyone," Rachel said. "And please don't be worried about your safety."

Loretta stood up, her long frame towering over Ruby, not that Ruby was short. "I feel better now having spoken with you, Rachel."

"Me, too," Ruby said.

The two women moved toward the door, but Ruby stopped to ask another question.

"Are Marc and Lola coming back here to live?"

Rachel hadn't even thought about that.

"I don't know, I guess so."

The elder women exchanged looks.

"Oh, boy," Ruby said as she walked through the doorway first.

FOURTEEN

THE THREE WOMEN sat at the clubhouse table. It was covered with trays of sweets. The chef was trying new recipes, and had decided Rachel and her friends were the perfect subjects to sample his deserts. Rachel reached for an éclair and took a huge bite. It tasted delicious, but didn't lift her spirits.

"Who is more stressed than me?" Rachel asked, lifting her iced tea glass high into the air. "I'll bet nobody."

"So, give us the skinny," Olivia said, daintily picking up a cherry tart and sipping from her glass.

"The last I heard from Detective France, he said that they had run out of leads."

"What?" Tia asked. "A woman was murdered in her own apartment and they can't find any evidence? That's crazy."

"There weren't any fingerprints, except for Eneida, Joe and me. However, there were two used wine glasses, meaning she had company, but the glasses were smashed and contaminated by the animals." Rachel looked disgusted as she sprinkled more sugar into her drink, stirring it with a straw. "So, Eneida knew the person who killed her. She let him —or her— into the condo willingly."

"That means it was an isolated incident," Olivia concluded. "We don't have a serial killer running amok in the complex. That part is good news."

"That's right, it was isolated. I wish people wouldn't go around spreading the rumor of a serial killer." Rachel sat up straight in her chair, clutching the armrests with both hands. "What I've had to deal with from these busybodies running around telling people there's a serial killer!"

"I heard that rumor," Tia said, reaching for a cookie. "I also heard that Marc killed Lola, but I saw her in the laundry room, so I knew that wasn't true."

"Yes, I heard something about Lola and Marc having a big fight and that he was the killer of Eneida," Olivia said.

"Oh, geez!! Not true!" Rachel slapped the armrests with both hands in frustration. "I hope when I get really old, I will have more to do than gossip."

"But wasn't Marc arrested?" Tia asked.

"Yes, but he was released because his lovely, loyal, dippy wife wouldn't testify against him." Rachel dropped her body back against the chair, releasing one hand from the armrest to get her drink. "Some women are so stupid."

"You don't understand abuse or you wouldn't say that," Tia said. "She's not stupid, Lola's needy, insecure, and scared."

"I do realize her character flaws and I understand that women such as Lola need help. And they're not stupid, I get it. I just wish she'd get some help," Rachel said in frustration with the situation. "I really do know Lola's not stupid. But I am tired of dealing with the aftermath of her fights with Marc." She finished off the éclair and reached for a tart.

"Has anyone attempted to get Lola some help?" Olivia suggested.

"According to Detective France, and my husband, she's unwilling."

"How so?" Tia asked, looking puzzled.

"When the feuding couple was brought into the station, Lola

claimed she loved her husband and that they didn't need any counseling. Life was good." Rachel stiffened her shoulders over that statement. "I guess some people think it's normal to be a punching bag."

"Lola hasn't developed the skills to see she doesn't have to live under those conditions," Tia said. "She was probably abused as a child or saw her mother being beaten. This is normal behavior to her."

"Well, if Joe ever smacked me around, he'd see some normal behavior out of me. I'd deck him," Rachel said.

"Because that isn't normal behavior to you," Tia said. "Lola doesn't have the strength at this time to recognize that she doesn't deserve to be beaten."

"Pitiful, just pitiful," Olivia said, shaking her head. "Well, I'm ready for another iced tea, and let's get more of these samples. Chef is such a nice guy. The least we can do is help him out. How about you girls?"

"No. I'd better go home because Joe is probably asleep and I don't want to disturb him," Rachel said to the server when she came to the table. "Besides, it's been a rough few days. I need sleep. But you can box a few of these for me?"

Rachel crept into the apartment as quietly as it was humanly possible. Scooting the throw rug to the side with her foot, she prepared to be pounced on. But nothing happened. All was quiet. Almost too quiet.

She slowly walked into the dining room, looking for Rufus. But there was no dog. Were the guys even home? It was eleven o'clock, way past Joe's bedtime. Maybe he was taking Rufus out for a walk, an emergency potty run? The door to the bedroom was partially open, so Rachel peeped around the corner. It was too dark to see anything and she couldn't turn on the light in case Joe was there actually sleeping.

As she pulled herself upright, Rachel stepped backwards, right onto Rufus's paw. *Yelp!* Rachel sprang forward and turned around. She reached down to comfort Rufus, who was more offended than hurt. He loved the attention he received, so he jumped on Rachel, trying to lick her face. Being in a crouched position, she lost her balance and fell backward into the door, sending it crashing into the wall. She landed on the floor with Rufus standing over her, giving her face a good washing. That's when the room lit up.

"Everything okay over there?" Joe asked from the far side of the bed.

"Huhhhh bluhhhh nuhhhh," Rachel tried to say with a mouth full of fur, still clutching and cradling the box full of sweets. "Un you huhhh mmmeeee."

Joe acted as if he understood what she had said. "Sure." He padded his bare feet around the corner of the bed and pulled Rufus away from Rachel.

"We can't keep doing this. Somebody's going to get hurt. Probably you," Joe said.

Rachel looked up from the floor at her husband. "You think? Maybe I'm hurt now."

"Only your pride," he said with a grin, extending his hand to help her up.

"You've got to teach that dog some manners," Rachel said, rubbing the back of her head. "He snuck up on me this time."

"I'll look into dog obedience classes tomorrow." Joe walked back to bed, stomping all the way.

"Good idea." Rachel went over to her closet. She removed her blouse, then her pants.

"Or you could stop drinking," Joe remarked from the bed.

She turned around wearing an expression daring him to make more comments. "Ooh. You didn't just say that?"

"Yes, I did. And I meant it." Joe was snuggled under the covers, with only his balding head protruding over top.

Rachel never anticipated he would have the nerve to carry on with his statement. She was taken back.

"You think I'm drinking, don't you?" She narrowed her eyes at him.

"Obviously, yes. And you do. Till late hours with the girls," Joe said, keeping his eyes closed as he lay on his back with workman's hands peeking from under the covers. "It's not becoming."

"Not becoming?" Rachel had never heard Joe say such a thing. "Not becoming for a woman? Not becoming for a wife? Not becoming for a condo manager? What?"

"Not becoming for you. You're a nice person. Unless you drink too much," he said, and then interrupted his conversation with a broad yawn. "Then your attitude shifts into the unbecoming."

Rachel stood still with her slacks dangling in her hands. She was stupefied. Joe never talked to her like that. Never. She didn't know how to respond.

"I think we should end this conversation," was all she could think to say.

"Fine with me. Good night." Joe rolled over to expose his back to her.

Rachel finished changing into her nightgown, brushed her teeth, and crawled into bed quietly beside Joe. Sleep didn't come for a while because she did not understand what was happening. She had not been drinking alcohol. Only iced tea.

By the time Rachel crawled out of bed the next morning, Joe had already left for work. From the looks of the kitchen, he hadn't bothered to eat breakfast. The coffee pot had not been used and no dirty dishes were in the sink. To add more mystery to the situation, she did not hear from or see Joe as of noon. That was unusual.

Ruby exited the double doors as she walked towards the pool. From his vantage point where he was working on the faulty watering hose,

Joe had a rear view of her bony hips sashaying around as she did her model walk.

"Hi, honey," Ruby said as she passed an old gentleman reclining in a chaise lounge. She tipped her hot pink sunhat back a bit and smiled. The old guy slapped a magazine over his face in response. She walked on.

Ruby spread her red lips into a friendly smile in front of the next elderly gentleman she encountered, cocking one hand on the exposed hip peeking over her hot pink bikini. She gave him her best model pose. "Hi, friend," Ruby said brightly.

The man looked at Ruby, speechless, his mouth agape. His lips twisted as if hunting for something to say, but came up short due to his apparent amazement over the brazenness of the woman standing in front of him.

"Oh, cat got your tongue? I'll bet you haven't seen anything like me before."

"No, ma'am, you are certainly an original," he finally managed to say. "Have a nice day."

"Your loss," Ruby said, sashaying herself away from him.

Rachel knew that newcomers to the building had an adjustment period when it came to Ruby. Nowhere had any of them encountered such an audacious personality. It took some longer than others to make the adjustment, if ever. Women found her boldness especially distasteful, so they never attempted friendship, especially if they were married, because the women were afraid Ruby would flirt with their husbands. However, that was never her intent. She just wanted attention and friendship. Consequently, the women missed the opportunity to know Ruby's kind heart. It may have been hidden under her bony chest and bold behavior, but it did exist. She had a soft spot for children and dogs. Ruby gave generously to the Halifax Humane Society and sponsored children so they could attend vacation Bible school. Her heart was as big as her outlandish behavior.

Ruby finally settled into a chaise lounge, right next to Rachel.

"Your day off?" Ruby asked.

"Yes, and a well-deserved one," Rachel said. She raised her body up so she could apply more suntan lotion, carefully avoiding the borders of her white full-piece suit.

"You having trouble sleeping?"

"What?" Rachel sat up straighter and looked over at the old woman. She never knew what was going to come out of her mouth.

"Lack of sleep will make you tired. And you're at that age where sleep can be a challenge. Night sweats, then you're freezing to death. I've been there." Ruby adjusted her hat so it covered more of her face, so as not to add to her collection of wrinkles.

Rachel pushed her sunglasses closer to her nose as she looked at Ruby. "I can't believe you just said that. Are you psychic or something?"

"Psychic has nothing to do with it. I'm in my nineties. I know these things."

"Well, I guess you must," Rachel said, reclining back into the chaise. "Going through menopause is causing my hormones to make my life miserable. By the way, I saw you flirting with those men."

Ruby chuckled. "I wasn't flirting. Why does everyone think I'm such a flirt? I'm just being friendly. I like people, for crying in the beer."

"Anyone ever take you up on your offer of friendship?"

"Oh, sure. Happens sometimes. Most times, no. They misinterpret my intent." Ruby sighed and relaxed her long body into the chaise.

Rachel thought Ruby's confession was a little sad. Everyone needs friends. But she knew the women in particular shunned the old woman out of jealousy.

"More power to you, Ruby. Don't give up. Besides, you don't need superficial friendships," she said, blotting her forehead with a towel. "And I'm your friend. Remember that."

"Thank you, Rachel."

She noticed a couple coming through the double doors, heading for the pool. It was Marc and Lola. Rachel was disgusted to see that they were holding hands.

"That's one slime ball over there," Ruby said, following Rachel's view. "I would never give him a moment of my time."

Marc and Lola must have felt the dislike coming from the two women because the couple sat as far from them as possible while still remaining by the pool. Lola was grinning up at her husband as if he were the greatest man in the world. He was being very charming with her in response, or else he was putting on a show for everyone.

"You letting them stay here?" Ruby asked with a tone of disapproval.

"I have to contact the couple that owns the condo. They have to be the ones who evict them."

"Well, don't wait until he decides he wants to take another crack at killing her again." With that advice, Ruby rolled over to sun her back.

After Rachel returned to her unit, she took a relaxing shower and slipped into comfy clothes. Her floaty tunic was all the confinement she wanted on this day.

She went to her desk and searched for the contact information on Margarita that she had been given by the detective. After finding the phone number for Eneida's daughter, Rachel dialed. As she sat in a chair, she heard a woman answer the phone.

"Hola?"

"Yes, Margarita, hello," she responded. "I am Rachel Barnes, a friend of your mother."

"Oh, yes, I remember," Margarita said, slipping into English to continue the conversation. "Mama mention you to me."

"Margarita, I am so sorry for your mother's death. It has been quite upsetting for me," Rachel said. "Please accept my condolences."

"Si, it has been upsetting. Gracias," she said in a heavy accent.

"How are you doing?" Rachel asked.

"I am sad in Miami."

Rachel thought she heard the woman's voice crack as she spoke.

"Is there anything I can do for you? Some way to help?"

"No," Margarita said, letting out a long sigh. "I arrange for cremation quick. I have her ashes here. She is at peace."

"That's very nice. Will you have a memorial for your mother?"

"Maybe, I don't know. Maybe not."

"If you decide to have one, please let me know." Rachel questioned if she would make the long drive down to Miami to attend, even if the daughter decided to arrange one.

"Si, I will do."

There was an awkward pause until Margarita spoke again.

"Do they know who killed my mother?"

The question rattled Rachel. This was such a tender issue for her. Of course, it was even more sensitive for Eneida's daughter. It was only natural for the young woman to want information and have the killer apprehended.

"Unfortunately, they do not know at this time," Rachel said. "There are no suspects."

"What about the man that visit her?"

"What man?" Rachel wasn't aware of any man who would have visited Eneida.

"My mama say a man came to visit her several times."

"I don't know anything about that."

"She say he not invited, just come," Margarita said. "She not like him."

"I see. Do you know who he was? Did she give you his name?"

"No, I not know. No name."

"Did she say if he lived in the building?"

"No say."

"Okay. I will inform the police that you knew of a man who visited her," Rachel said. "Maybe that will help with the investigation."

"Si, I hope."

The two women ended their conversation, promising to keep in touch. Rachel knew that wouldn't happen. It was just something said in situations like this. But at least she gained some information to help with the investigation. Something good came from their conversation. Perhaps a lead to the killer. Rachel called Detective France immediately with the news.

FIFTEEN

"I'M glad you had the idea," Rachel said as she drove. "I could kick myself for not having thought of it myself."

"You've been busy," Olivia said as she adjusted her seatbelt more comfortably on her shoulder. "Do you know where you're going?"

"Yes, it's been a while, but I remember the way. The shelter is in the country near New Smyrna Beach," Rachel said. "Practically in no man's land."

"I was just concerned that maybe the poor cats hadn't been adopted. Eneida always took home the most pathetic cases, the least adoptable." Olivia adjusted her sunglasses as she snuggled into the seat. "I love cats. They are my personal favorite, yet I don't have any."

"Her cats are probably still there. Don't get upset if we find them. At least they won't be killed like in other shelters," Rachel said, making a hard right turn into a less populated area. "How's your love life?"

Olivia's smile lit up her pretty skin. She fussed with her necklace a moment before answering. "Since you asked, it's doing very well. We've gone out a bunch of times since he got back from the conference."

"A bunch? He hasn't been back that long."

Olivia's giggle in response struck Rachel as amusing. "We've been out to dinner every night," she said, sounding almost embarrassed. "I'm going to get fat from all this dating."

"Every night? Well, things are moving along rapidly, I'd say."

"Yes, they are. And I'm so happy."

Rachel could see joy beaming all over Olivia's face. It made her feel good to see her friend so happy.

"Is he allergic to cats?" Rachel asked.

"What?" Olivia's head rotated around sharply in Rachel's direction.

"You're going to be tempted to adopt one of Eneida's cats when you see them. So, is he allergic?" Rachel asked as she maneuvered her vehicle around a turtle in the road.

"I don't know. The subject hasn't come up for discussion. I don't think he has any pets because he works long hours," Olivia said, looking puzzled.

"If he is, he can take medication then," Rachel said.

"Hmm, I guess so." Olivia relaxed back into her seat, perhaps contemplating a new addition.

After a little more time, Rachel turned into a driveway. "This is it."

They drove down a dirt road that led to a wooden building that stretched across the entrance. It was an old, one story building, but it had recently been painted. The telltale paint cans were still nearby, waiting to be put away. They heard dogs barking around the other side of the building.

"We're being greeted," Olivia said as she exited the car.

"The cat area is that building over there," Rachel said, pointing in the appropriate direction. "I wonder where Jorge is?"

As if on cue, Jorge appeared at the edge of the building.

"Welcome!" His broad smile showed large teeth and his eyes crinkled from years working outside. He was Puerto Rican, on the short side, and a bit wide around the middle. Jorge removed his straw hat politely and reached his hand out to the women.

"I'm Rachel and this is Olivia," Rachel said as she clasped his hand. "I don't know if you remember me?"

"I remember." Jorge's smile did not fade. "Nice to meet you," he said to Olivia.

"We came to see the cats that you picked up from the Humane Society. The ones belonging to Eneida." Jorge's face lost its joy. He fumbled his hands around his hat and cast his head down, then turned around, still with his head bent.

"Follow me," he said.

The two women exchanged looks, both recognizing his distress, but followed silently as Jorge led the way to the cattery.

"They are still here," he said after they entered the building. "They are not young. The white one is not what people want. She's over there," he said, pointing to a cage.

"Oh, she's beautiful," Olivia said, immediately gravitating over to the feline's cage. "Such a lovely girl," she cooed. Pale blue eyes stared back at her, then the cat rubbed her body against the bars.

"Oh, Rachel, she's wooing me!"

"The boys are here," Jorge said, patting the larger cage where two ebony cats sat looking out at the humans approaching. "They're good guys."

Jorge turned around, looking bleak. Rachel studied the man, noting his emotional nature. He obviously cared a great deal about Eneida and her cats.

"Tell me, Jorge, has there been any interest in the cats?" Rachel asked, knowing the answer.

"None."

"No one wants these beautiful babies?" Olivia asked.

"No one."

"That is just not acceptable," Olivia stated firmly. She raised her shoulders high and looked over to Rachel. "We have to do something."

"What are you suggesting?" Rachel already had Sasquatch taking up residence.

"How many cats am I allowed to have according to the rules of the condo association?" Olivia all but stamped her foot in her determination to right a wrong.

Rachel immediately saw where this situation was headed. "Two."

"Then you have to take one. I'll take two," Olivia said.

When Rachel's eyes widened, Olivia became more forceful. "We have to do this for Eneida. She would want this to happen. We can't leave these cats here."

"But there are other cats here as well. We can't take them all home." Rachel was getting concerned. She had Joe to consider, and he wasn't in her corner at the moment.

"Of course. But we can at least take home those Eneida had. You know she would want us to," Olivia said. "We can't leave them here."

"As I asked you before, does your beau have allergies to cats?" Rachel looked her friend squarely in the face, as if she thought she had a chance of reasoning with her.

"It doesn't matter. He can just take a pill if he does." Obviously, there was no persuading Olivia from her mission.

"Okay, well, I guess that settles that. So, which two do you want?" Rachel asked.

"I want the white one and one of the black boys. Sort of like dominos. Ivory and ebony." She stood back with her arms folded over her ample chest. "You take the other black one."

"Thanks. Joe is going to kill me for sure." Rachel threw up her arms in surrender. "Deal."

"We didn't bring any carriers with us," Olivia said.

"I can provide," Jorge said, a little smile pulling at his lips.

"Of course, we'll return them," Rachel said.

"Okay," Jorge said, now all smiles once again. "You need litter box?"

"Oh, a litter box!" Rachel hadn't thought that far.

"We can pick up two on the way home," Olivia said.

"Good thought," Rachel said. "And litter."

While they waited for Jorge to find three carriers, Rachael considered the man who ran the rescue operation. He appeared to be a loner. Who else would willingly live within an animal shelter compound? Eneida had, but she owned the place. She had been fortunate to discover Jorge. He loved animals and was gentle with all of them. The shelter couldn't have been in better hands.

"Eneida will be so happy," Olivia said when the man returned with the carriers.

Rachel and Jorge looked at Olivia strangely.

"You know what I mean. She's looking down on us, she knows." Olivia strutted off with a big smile on her face.

"Hey, maybe we can convince Tia to take one cat?" Rachel offered to Olivia's back. "She just might do it."

"Not mine," Olivia said.

Now Rachel felt guilty. What was she to do? Appear not as good a friend to Eneida as Olivia for not taking one cat, or take one and totally risk angering Joe? Sometimes life choices are not easy...Joe would just have to be angry.

Later, Rachel walked into her apartment pushing a cart with the cat carrier, a litter box, litter, and cat food. Joe wasn't home, much to her relief. But Rufus was.

The dog immediately zoned in on the carrier with the new addition inside. Rufus ferociously sniffed all around the cage, risking getting his snout soundly smacked by a paw full of claws.

"Okay, knock it off, Rufus," she said. "Get used to it. You know this cat, so back off."

One spit from the cat sent the dog backing up.

"Woosy," Rachel said. "Or smart, not sure which." She left the two animals to get reacquainted.

Rachel guessed Joe would be home soon, so she started working on dinner after she found a place for the litter box in the second bathroom. She was starving. The thought crossed her mind that she'd be wise to make something special to soothe Joe's annoyance with her and the addition of a new animal. Suddenly, they had gone from none to two, and one was a handful. She pulled out a steak from the freezer, placing it in the microwave to defrost. A Caesar salad sounded like a good choice to accompany the steak. And chocolate cake for dessert, not that either one of them needed it.

After about an hour, Rachel allowed the cat the opportunity to explore its new surroundings. Boldly, he walked right under Rufus' nose on his way to investigate the master bedroom. The dog's tail was wagging as he intently sniffed the path being created. The cat's trek next led to the bathroom, followed by the guest bedroom and bath. He took a couple good sniffs at the litter box, evidently approving it. Once the side rooms were explored, the cat walked around the living and dining rooms, sniffing along. Last was the kitchen. His little nose twitched at the tantalizing smells wafting about.

"We have to name you, don't we?" Rachel looked down at the jet black cat. "Smoky? Blackie? No, too obvious. I'll have to think about it. Maybe Joe will have a good name."

While she was shaking some croutons on the salad, Joe entered the apartment.

"Hello?"

"Right here in the kitchen," Rachel answered.

Joe peered into the kitchen at his wife. "I'm sorry."

"What do you have to be sorry about?" Rachel stopped shaking out croutons, her hand poised in midair.

"I was rude last night. I all but called you an alcoholic, and I'm sorry for that," he said, looking down at his dirty boots. "And you deserve to spend time with your friends."

"Joe, you don't need to apologize," she said, turning around to face him. "I was wrong. It was all me, not you at all. You have a right to feel as you do, but I..."

"Well, I could have been kinder." He interrupted her words.

"I think you were plenty kind, Joe." Rachel threw her hands into the air. "I was not kind, or understanding of you. And I do seem to have a reaction after I've been out with the girls. That can't continue as it's been. I don't know why I get so ornery and stubborn over simple things. I'm sorry." She also needed to investigate into why she felt drunk after drinking iced tea. That was just crazy.

"What the..." Joe said when he discovered a cat rubbing against his pants leg. Then Rufus plowed into him in hot pursuit of the cat, the only thing that would have delayed his greeting of Joe. After almost knocking him over, Rufus jumped up, paws positioned on his chest. The cat let out a loud meow below as if he were saying hello to his new daddy, all the while rubbing Joe's leg. So, of course, the dog had to chime in with a couple soft woofs.

"Down, Rufus. Who are you?" Joe looked down at his feet to watch the black cat rubbing all over him. "And where did you come from?" Looking up at Rachel, he said, "Someone has some explaining to do."

"That's one of Eneida's cats. Olivia and I went to the shelter today," she said, wiping her hands on her apron. "I knew Olivia would want to take home at least one of the cats, but I never dreamed I'd get talked into taking one as well. Actually, she took two."

"I see," he said, staring at the cat at his ankles. "What's its name?"

"I don't know. I was hoping for suggestions from you."

"Oh, so you didn't think I'd object?" Now he was looking at her again.

"Well, I hoped you'd be okay with him. He is a boy. And I couldn't leave him there when Olivia took two. A black one and a white one." She stared pitifully at him, hoping he'd relent.

Rufus let out another soft woof.

"I don't see any reason we shouldn't keep him. As long as we aren't breaking any rules," he said.

"No rules broken. Oh, terrific, Joe!" She took two steps and threw her arms around her husband. "Thank you for being so kind and understanding. I need to take lessons from you."

Joe laughed and kissed his wife on the lips.

"Benny," Joe said, after he drew back.

"Benny what?"

"Benny is his name."

"Oh. Benny. That sounds pretty good," she said. "Do you like the name Benny?" she asked the cat, which was now twirling in and out of both their legs.

"Purp," answered the cat.

"Come on, Benny, let's feed you," Rachel said, turning away from Joe. "And you, too, Rufus. I can't exclude you."

After a wonderful steak dinner, Rachel was reading in bed, propped up with two pillows. Joe was beside her watching TV, clicking different channels with the remote. He couldn't find anything interesting. About the time he settled on an old Law and Order episode, Benny decided to join them. He popped easily onto the bed and then padded over toward Rachel.

"Meow."

"Meow yourself," Rachel said, not turning away from the page she was reading. Benny was being loving, rubbing against her hand, jarring the book. Then he rubbed her arms until he discovered her hair. One paw raised to comb her hair with his claws.

"Ow! Benny!"

The next thing they knew, Rufus came to the rescue. All one hundred pounds of yellow fur jumped onto the center of the bed. Rachel's book was knocked from her hands, falling to the floor. Benny jumped onto the headboard, which was a narrow strip of wood. Trying to balance precariously, the cat looked for an escape from Rufus. But the dog had other ideas. He rose one paw next to Benny, making soft growling noises. He wasn't intending to hurt the cat, just communicate. Or play. Or whatever. Benny took exception to this behavior and hissed at the dog, taking a little smack at his nose. Rufus let out a whine.

Joe decided he needed to intervene, while Rachel was trying to get out of the way.

"Rufus, leave the cat alone!" Joe said, rolling over to grab his collar.

The cat took this opportunity to leap away, first bouncing onto

Rachel's head, then onto the night stand. As Benny made a run for it, he bumped the lamp, sending it flying to the floor. The lamp made a loud thump before it broke. Joe kept trying to wriggle Rufus off the bed on the other side. Of course, the dog wouldn't go gently. He was determined to be the only animal in the bed. Joe pulled on his collar, finally convincing the dog to get off the bed. But not before his swishing tail connected with the glass of water Joe had on his night stand, sending it crashing to the floor.

"Joe! The neighbors underneath will think we're having a fight," Rachel said.

"Well, it looks like we are," he said, glancing around the room.

Broken glass was on both sides of the bed and the covers were ripped half off, dangling on the floor.

"My poor lamp!" Rachel cried, looking over at the damage.

"I'll get the broom," Joe said. "Don't walk on the glass with your bare feet."

While at the closet, he noticed the animals had quieted down. A little too quiet. With a broom and dust pan in hand, he went exploring and found the two brats in the guest bedroom, comfortably resting on the double bed. Rufus was lounging, with Benny snuggled up between his two front legs. Both looked innocently back at him.

"I'll be darned."

Joe returned to his bedroom and swept up the broken glass and mumbling, “Is this a preview of coming events?”

SIXTEEN

LORETTA ENTERED RACHEL'S OFFICE, standing briefly in the doorway as if she were being presented at a ball, looking sophisticated, as usual, in a deep blue pantsuit. No one would have ever suspected she had once been a police detective in Nevada because her appearance gave every indication of her being a classy, God-fearing woman, possibly in society.

"Good morning, Loretta," Rachel said. "You look lovely."

"Thank you, dear. I have my association fee here," she said, handing over a check.

"Do you want a receipt?"

"No, the check is fine as a receipt."

"Loretta, may I ask you a personal question?"

"That depends on the question," Loretta said with a slight smile. She moved over to the chair.

"I understand. It isn't a secret that you were once a high-profile detective in Nevada," Rachel said.

Loretta looked steadily at Rachel, unflustered. "That is correct, although you and I have never discussed my past."

"What was it like being a detective?"

Loretta's face broke out in a smile and she laughed. "Oh, I would say at best it was an adventure. At worst, it was dangerous. I met many notable, influential people. All walks of life filter into and out of Nevada. Some were nonviolent offenders, while others were quite dangerous and cruel. Most had big bank accounts."

"The notables were...?"

"Famous people, wealthy people, politicians. Everyone comes to Nevada to gamble, you know," Loretta said. "We had to be discreet and careful during investigations, otherwise, we could become victims."

"You mean, be killed?"

"Of course." Loretta said that with such calm, like it was an understood consequence.

Rachel sat back in her chair to contemplate that thought.

"Rich, famous men who are participating in illegal enterprises do not want their wives knowing where the money is coming from. Those business trips they were supposed to be on were frequently to negotiate drug deals, money laundering, high scale theft, you name it." Loretta seemed easy divulging this information. "And the politicians, well, their constituents certainly couldn't know about their activities, now could they?"

"No, I guess not. So, you learned to be cautious."

"I did, quickly." She folded her elegant hands in her lap, steadily gazing at Rachel.

"You really could write a book, Loretta." Rachel's eyes crinkled at the thought. "It would be a guaranteed best seller."

"Yes, it most certainly would. But I'd be dead for doing so."

"I can understand that potential. Tell me, why does Ruby seem to hate you so much? Is she jealous? Or maybe she disapproves of your former profession?" Rachel shook her head in question.

Loretta's eyes fell to her lap. Now she appeared uncomfortable.

"You don't have to tell me. It's okay, forget I asked," Rachel said.

Immediately she grabbed her fan from the desk and began fanning herself out of necessity and to distract.

"No, I don't mind answering your question," she said, raising her eyes. "I trust you won't tell anyone, except maybe your husband."

"Of course not. I won't say anything to anyone." Rachel fanned away.

"Ruby used to work for me."

"As a detective?"

"No. She was an informant."

"Ruby was a Confidential Informant?"

"Yes. And she was very good at it," Loretta said. "Being a fashion model, she met many wealthy and influential men. She was such a beauty when she was young, always being invited to the best parties and feature events in Nevada."

"I see."

"Ruby had connections I could never have hoped to acquire. She rubbed elbows with the elite because she was a top model. What she would casually overhear at a party was invaluable information that no one else could have gained being on the police force. And what she found out for me in a clandestine manner was priceless."

Loretta looked steadily at Rachel, possibly judging her reaction to the conversation they were having. Rachel thought she was handling it well, except for the vigorous fanning of herself.

"Ruby was one of your informants," Rachel was finally able to say. "That's quite a shocker."

"And she doesn't want anyone to know about her past," Loretta said. "She moved to Florida to get away from me and the potential fallout from the criminals who might want to see me dead for arresting them. She didn't want any of them seeking her out and killing her once they were released from prison. So, when I happened to move here and she discovered I was a new resident, she thought her secret would be out. But I haven't said anything to anyone, except you."

"Well, that explains a lot," Rachel said.

"Ruby doesn't really hate me, she's just concerned I might tell her secret. If word gets out about her, maybe some crook from the past will come looking for her. Who knows? I have assured her I won't say anything to anyone who might prove dangerous, but she doesn't believe me, so she lives in fear of being exposed and fear of criminals finding her as well," Loretta said. "She usually keeps her distance from me, which is a shame. We used to be close."

"Wow, this is amazing news. I can hardly believe what I've heard," Rachel said, sinking further into her chair.

"You can't tell Ruby. She has to tell you herself. Which might be never."

"I won't say a word, I promise." Rachel had another question now. "Was she a C.I. for a long time? I mean, did she work for you for years or, I don't know..."

"She worked for me for about five years, and then faded into the woodwork. Ruby is a little older than me, so her days as a model were limited. She eventually had to give up that lifestyle and move on, which she did. I'm really not sure where she went after that or when she came to Florida. I hadn't seen her in many years, until I moved here."

"Was she always a redhead?"

Loretta threw her head back and let out a burst of laughter. "Yes, she always had red hair. It's obvious she still dyes it. At her age, the only color up there now is snow white."

"We just never know who lives among us, do we?"

"We sure don't, Rachel. Who would have thought I'd live in Florida, on the beach, in a condo after living in the desert? Certainly not me." Loretta rose from the chair a little creakily. "I better be going now. It was nice chatting with you, dear."

"Oh, it was my pleasure spending time with you, Loretta." Rachel escorted the woman to the door. "Take care."

As Loretta was half way through the door, she partially turned around toward Rachel. "You might try Evening Primrose Oil for those hot flashes, my dear."

"Okay, thanks for the tip."

"And cut down on that caffeine."

"Yes, ma'am."

Loretta left the office.

Ruby, a Confidential Informant. Wow! Wait till I tell Joe!

SEVENTEEN

"THAT CAT IS RUBBING up against my leg," Joe said as he sat at the table, attempting to eat his dinner.

"Maybe he likes you," Rachel said as she sliced up a tomato. "And his name is Benny."

Joe was looking down at Benny being busy. "Maybe he's rubbing off his fleas."

"He doesn't have fleas. He simply likes you," Rachel insisted.

"Why can't he rub his fleas on you at the dinner table?"

Rachel looked up from her plate and put down her utensils. "You don't like the cat?"

"I didn't exactly say that."

"You sort of did." Rachel picked up her iced tea and took a sip. "What was I to do? I was caught in a pickle. Besides, he's pretty. The dog likes him."

"Rufus likes everybody and thing. He's not a good character reference."

"So, would you prefer that I take the cat back to the shelter?" She was staring at him now, watching him put a bite of pork chop into his mouth. "Hmm?"

"No. The cat can't go back to the shelter." Joe was firm about that. "No more shelter for Benny."

"So, what's the problem?" Rachel resumed eating.

"I don't know...He's black. He's spooky. He sneaks around."

"All cats sneak around when there's a giant dog in the house. And what's with the prejudice against black cats?"

Joe looked at her like she had sprouted green hair. "I'm not prejudiced against his *color*!"

"Some people are afraid of black cats. Which is ridiculous, I might add," Rachel said, picking up her glass again. "Olivia took the white cat, or we could have had that one."

"I don't care what color the cat is. Black is beautiful. I take back what I said. The cat is fine, Benny stays, end of discussion," Joe said.

"But you said..."

"Forget what I said, it's fine. Eat your dinner."

Rachel restrained her normal eye roll. *Men are so peculiar.*

Later that evening, Rachel sat at her dressing table in the bathroom, eyeing her chin. She rummaged around until she found her tweezers and started plucking hairs.

Joe came into the bathroom to brush his teeth, looking sideways as he passed her.

"What are you doing?"

"Plucking out hairs."

"You mean you have whiskers?" Joe cocked his head to the side as he stared at Rachel.

"Whiskers! No, these are unruly hairs," she said, pulling one out with a grimace. "Well, they are a bit coarse. Maybe they are whiskers."

"Since when do women grow whiskers?"

"Since menopause, Joe. We get hair where we never had it before, hot flashes, cold chills, mood swings, you name it. All thanks to mother nature." She plucked another hair.

"All thanks to getting older," Joe said, moving along to one of the sinks. Rachel stopped plucking long enough to shoot him a sideways glare.

"Yes, Joe, it is. Just like you losing hair on your head and gaining it all over your ears," she remarked with a slight grin.

Joe rubbed his hand across the top of his head. What once had been a thick head of hair was now decidedly thin. The woes of growing older.

"So, you're sure about the new addition?" Rachel asked.

"Which one? We have Rufus and the cat." Joe squeezed toothpaste on his brush and stuck it into his mouth.

"The cat, of course. Are you okay with calling him Benny?"

"Well, there's always Blackie," he slurred in between brushing.

"Can't we be a little more original, huh?"

"Soot." Except when he said the word it came out as shut.

"No."

"Coal."

Rachel turned toward him. "No. Get serious."

"I don't know. I'm named out. You choose," he said, toothbrush out of his mouth.

"Schwarz," she threw out to him.

Joe turned around to look at her after sliding his toothbrush back into the holder. "What is that?"

"It's German for black."

"Schwarz?"

"Yes, I looked it up."

"Well, if you've already decided, why ask me?"

"I was giving you an opportunity to participate."

"Schwarz? Really?"

"Yes."

Joe walked out of the bathroom, calling back to his wife, "Schwarz, s'mores, whatever you want, I don't care. But I prefer Benny."

Rachel sat on her chair, plucking and grinning. "Then Benny it remains," she said.

. . .

Lola and Marc were acting like a newlywed couple every time they were in public. At the pool they held hands, smooched a little, and lovingly rubbed suntan lotion on each other's backs, all the while with big smiles on their faces. Everyone thought it was a farce. But Lola did look very happy. She was the only one residing in the entire condominium who believed the romantic scenes playing out before one and all.

Rachel had heard rumors that Lola was telling people how sweet Marc was to her, that they had reconciled, and all was well. Rachel didn't believe it. Marc was biding his time until he struck again, like a cat teasing its prey. One good thing, Joe had taken note that their garbage receptacle was overflowing, which was a positive sign that they were cleaning up their mess.

Detective France paid a visit to Rachel's office. It was late Friday afternoon, and Rachel was eager to leave on time. But with his arrival, that wasn't likely.

"Hope I'm not interrupting you," the detective said as he poked his head inside the door to her office.

"Oh, no, come right in!" Rachel greeted him warmly, despite her eagerness to leave.

"I thought I would give you an update," he said, lowering his fit body into the chair. "We had an anonymous report about someone seen in your complex who didn't belong."

"What? Who? I mean, when? I don't understand."

"A couple days after the murder, a man in a dark coat and hat was seen trying to enter through the doors. Apparently, he was unsuccessful," France said. "Whoever saw him, felt he did not belong here because, in this person's opinion, he looked suspicious. The man tried the door several times and kept looking around for another entry."

"That is strange. Who wears a coat and hat in Daytona Beach?"

"He also attempted to call someone on the house phone to be buzzed in, but that didn't work out. What do you make of it?" France asked.

"I have no idea," Rachel said. "If we had a security camera, we might gain some answers. With the murder and suspicious people lurking about, I probably need to install some cameras."

"That would be my suggestion."

"I need to share something with you," Rachel said, edging her chair closer to the desk. "I had a conversation with a former police detective from Nevada. A high-profile detective."

France looked surprised and interested. "Really? High-profile? How did you come to converse with someone like that?"

"She lives here. And that's not for public knowledge."

"Holy crow, you never know, do you?" He grinned at Rachel. "You run quite the place here, don't you think?"

Rachel failed to see the humor. "She's a very nice, respectable woman. Goes to church and all. But her past is definitely interesting, yes." Rachel leaned closer toward France over her desk. "I had the thought that perhaps...who knows...maybe someone was looking for her? Not that I said that to her."

"The suspicious man."

"Exactly."

"Is she currently aware of anyone wanting to do her harm?" France asked. "Has she received any threats?"

"I don't think so. She never indicated such when I spoke with her. And that was recently," she said.

"That's not much to go on. But I'll make note of it," he said.

“Did anything come about regarding the visitor to Eneida’s unit?”

“Nothing conclusive, but we have it to consider should other information come up.”

“Of course.”

"And you, please install some security cameras in this place!" France said as he stood to leave

"Yes, sir! Right away, sir!" Rachel smiled at France. "Seriously, I will take care of it immediately."

After the detective left, Rachel took the time to call a security firm she knew of. They would arrive in the morning, she was told. One less stress off her heaping plate of anxiety.

EIGHTEEN

"OKAY, I want a chocolate bar. A big one." Rachel said rather loudly. "I'm not going home until I have at least one."

"Since when are you into chocolate?" Olivia said, sending Rachel a peculiar look. "I'll have an iced tea," she said to the server. Then pointing to Rachel, "And she'll have one, too."

"I'll third that," Tia chimed in. Turning to the women, she said, "It's been a rough day. If I have one more woman complain to me about menopause, I'm going to puke."

Mental note to self, Rachel thought, *don't grumble about hot flashes*.

"Tomorrow I am having security cameras installed at various places around the complex," Rachel announced.

"Good idea, after the murder," Olivia said.

"You should have had that done sooner," Tia remarked.

"You're right, I should have. But I didn't." Rachel allowed the server to place her iced tea and a plate of cookies in front of her. He followed it with a bowl of chocolate truffles. Rachel took a handful.

"If we have another incident where someone gets hurt, the cameras will be essential," Olivia said, accepting her drink.

"True, and necessary in this time of crime," commented Tia, accepting her tea as well.

Rachel took a sip from her glass, swirled the straw around twice to dissolved the sugar bags she poured in, and said, "A suspicious man was seen trying to get into the building recently."

Both women shifted their eyes over to Rachel. "What?" they said in unison.

Rachel nodded her head. "I'm afraid it's true," she said, taking a full swallow of her drink. "But it could be unrelated to the murder. It could be totally innocent."

"Or it could be someone coming back to get the intended victim because Eneida wasn't the one they wanted," Olivia said.

"And then there's that," Rachel said. "Hence, the installation of security cameras."

"Life is so dangerous now. I don't like this," said Tia.

"Remind you of India?" Olivia asked.

"Frightfully so," Tia said.

"Hey, we're not in India, not in New York City or Detroit. We're in sunny Daytona Beach, ladies," Rachel said in an attempt to rouse her friends. "Crime is not a big deal here. Yes, we have an occasional murder and so forth, but it would be so much worse elsewhere in a bigger city. Lighten up!" Rachel took two big gulps of her drink to wash down the truffles.

Silence fell over the table of friends as they contemplated this new reality of danger at their condo. A loud thunder boom sounded, interrupting the silence and a touch of ozone filled the air.

"Here we go again," Tia said. "When I came downstairs from my unit, it was roaring hot and sunny. Now we get a storm."

"Every day without fail," Olivia said. "The weather amazes me."

"Yes, how it can be raining on one side of the street and not the other," Rachel said. "Or how a storm will breeze through and then it's sunny again. Crazy weather." She stood.

"Where are you going?" Olivia asked.

"To get that candy bar I was talking about. I have to have some more chocolate." Rachel left the table to find the snack machine near the restrooms. She returned quickly with two chocolate bars.

"I thought you only wanted one?" Olivia said. "You ate all the truffles, too."

Rachel looked down at the empty bowl.

I guess I did.

"They're small, so I got two." Rachel quickly peeled off the wrapper on one and popped a portion of the bar into her mouth.

"You're going to gain weight if you keep eating those," Tia said.

"Actually, they seem to be having the opposite effect," Rachel said. "I'm losing weight."

Tia raised her eyebrows. "Keep an eye on that weight loss. It could mean something."

"I doubt it."

Boom! Crash! Lightning lit up the clubhouse.

The women never stopped talking.

"Olivia, how's your romance going?" Tia asked.

That's all Tia had to say. Olivia's color brightened from her chest up to her forehead. She also beamed and smiled in response.

"Oh, life is just amazing!" Her hands were swaying in the air now. "I am just one happy girl. My beau is wonderful, caring, and such a gentleman."

"Ooh, sounds like the girl's in love," Rachel said.

"Are you in love?" asked Tia.

"Yes. I'm in love with Ronald." As if her skin weren't red enough already, her coloring went up a few degrees.

"Honey, your face looks like a red balloon," Rachel said, smiling.

"Okay, we've talked seriously," Olivia began, "and he has been hinting at a more permanent relationship."

"Like moving in together?" Rachel asked.

"Yes."

"What did you say?" Tia asked.

"I'm supposed to be thinking about it." Olivia fussed around with her collar, which was a sure sign she was uneasy.

She cast her big brown eyes on Rachel and then Tia and sighed. "I don't particularly want to live with Ronald, or any other man for that matter. I enjoy living by myself. After raising four kids without a father, I am thrilled to be able to do exactly as I please, when I please, and then decide to do the complete opposite. Just because I can."

"Oh." The two ladies said in unison.

"And if I'm going to live with a man, he's going to be my husband," Olivia said, heaving another sigh. "Yes, that's old fashioned, I know. But that's who I am."

"Have you shared that bit of news with Ronald?" Tia asked

"Not yet. It's not an easy topic to bring up," Olivia said. "It's also too soon to discuss marriage. But with his long hours, we could see each other more frequently if I were conveniently living in his house."

"Yes, that's a pickle to be in," said Rachel, chewing on her candy bar.

"Well, I say, stay where you are if you're happy living by yourself," Tia said. "Besides, why do you have to move? Why can't he move?"

"He has a big house, so he won't move into a two-bedroom condo," Olivia said. "And I don't expect him to."

"The house trumps the condo," Rachel said, waving at the server. "I understand that. Maybe one of you will come up with an alternative plan."

"There's no rush," Tia said, nodding to the server that she also wanted a drink.

"No rush. I agree," Olivia said, shaking her head no to another drink. "Ladies, I have some paperwork to do before classes resume after summer break, so I'm off."

"Oh, so soon?" Tia asked.

"We'll miss you." Rachel gave her a sad face.

"We can catch up next week," Olivia said, reaching down for her purse. "But I need to go."

"Bye," the ladies called out to Olivia.

. . .

Olivia snuggled into the couch under a throw blanket she kept handy to keep her feet warm. For some reason, ever since menopause set in, her feet were always cold. She tucked in the cover around her legs as well. Feeling satisfied, Olivia opened the Bible sitting in her lap. Maybe she could find some answers in here. It wasn't long before the two cats came to settle in on either side of her.

"Hi, babies." They responded with soft purrs. The crashing outside didn't seem to bother them.

The white one loved to rub incessantly on the blanket, thus leaving lots of white hair clinging to it. The black one was content to lean into Olivia and purr. She had decided to name the white one Pearl and the black one Ebony. They were adjusting nicely, probably because they had each other as company.

Olivia realized that her friends didn't understand about her hesitation to move in with Ronald. She knew they didn't understand because they weren't religious. Tia had been a Hindu, but didn't appear to practice any religion now. Rachel, on the other hand, had a loose relationship with God. She rarely attended church, although Joe did. When she did attend it was at the behest of Joe because it was a holiday. She was one of those Easter and Christmas attendees.

Olivia flipped open the Bible to Psalms, searching for guidance.

NINETEEN

BY THE TIME Rachel arrived at her front door, she had downed two chocolate bars, a half-dozen cookies, ten truffles and several iced teas. She was definitely feeling high. Her steps were rocky and her hand had difficulty locating the keyhole. It was way past dinner, so she didn't know what Joe had eaten, or even if he had. Maybe he was asleep. She rather hoped he was. He wouldn't be happy with her in her present condition. Plus, she was feeling ornery for some reason. This was something he didn't need to know.

Rattling the keys to gain entry, Rachel was surprised when the door swung open. While she anticipated an attack from Rufus, she wondered why the front door wasn't locked. She shut the door, but still there was nothing moving around her. No sound. No clinking dog tags. Rachel didn't know if she had skated an attack or what had happened? She flipped on the light and saw – nothing. The light didn't go on. That reality annoyed her. Why hadn't Joe changed the light bulb? How was she to find her way around in the dark and not be attacked by Rufus? She was surely at the dog's mercy now. And why hadn't Joe locked the front door?

"Weird. Or I'm lucky." She wasn't sure.

Rachel took one step forward in the dark and tripped on the carpeting. She fell to the floor and felt pain at her knee. "Ugh, why am I such a klutz?" she mumbled.

As she was trying to get up from the carpet in the dark, Rachel suddenly remembered, there wasn't any carpeting in her unit. It had wooden floors. The surface under her hands was definitely carpet. "Holy Moly, where am I?"

Feeling disoriented as she stood, Rachel turned to where she thought the front door was located, pushing out her hands to feel for it. She took several steps before realizing she hadn't walked that far originally.

"Where are you, door?"

Rachel began to cry, even sobbing a little after she again tripped over her feet. Swaying around, she managed to keep upright.

"Okay, I get it. I'm a bad girl tonight. But please, help me find the door!"

Rachel heard a noise she recognized as coming from the elevator, so she turned in that direction, carefully taking baby steps toward the sound. Once she felt the door, she reached below for the knob and opened it. Stepping into the walkway, she turned around to look at the number of the unit on the door. 810. This was Eneida's unit. She wasn't even on the correct floor. Quickly locking the door, she returned to the elevator. Rachel punched her floor button, feeling like a fool. She had no intention of telling anyone about this.

Finally arriving at her unit on the fourth floor, Rachel was relieved to find no one home. Joe and Rufus must have been out for an emergency walk because the leash was missing from the hook by the door. Rachel placed her purse on the dining room table, but knocked it over, the contents spilling out. Getting down on her knees, she discovered her right knee hurt. Looking at her knee, she saw a gash zipping across the kneecap and blood oozing out.

"Stupid. How stupid."

She sat down beside the contents that had been in her purse and began to gather up the items that had fallen out. Lipstick, compact, check book, wallet, everything was in a pile. She heard keys jingling as she started to rise with her items in hand. Suddenly feeling faint, she couldn't get her balance, so she fell back down. The front door opened to reveal Joe and the dog coming in from their walk. There was Rachel, seated on the floor with her items in hand, staring at Joe and the dog. After being released from the leash, Rufus immediately ran over to where Rachel sat. Then the dog did what Rufus did best: he lunged toward Rachel, easily knocking her backwards from her seated position. Rufus promptly straddled Rachel, licking her face and head. She protested, but it did no good. She tried to rise, but the dog decided to plop all of his weight on her body. No way she could get up now. Breathing was an issue.

"Get up! Get off me!" she whispered breathlessly.

"Come here, Rufus," Joe said. "Be a good boy."

The dog rose and came to Joe.

"Good boy!" Joe said, patting his head.

Rachel raised her head to look at the two of them. She knew her hair was a crazy mess, half in her face. She grumbled as she moved her body into a kneeling position, and then finally stood, wobbling. The items from her purse were still on the floor, but she chose to not gather them up. Trying to muster some dignity, she put her hands on her hips.

"You're a mess," Joe observed.

"Well, what do you expect after being attacked by Sasquatch?"

"I expect you wouldn't have been in that position if you weren't drunk." He made his statement evenly, without a raised voice.

"I'm not drunk," she argued.

"You're swaying; you can't stand up right; and you look drunk," he said. "I can see it in your face. I can smell it. Rotten fruit on your breath. Gin?"

Rachel didn't respond. She just swayed a little more.

Joe walked away, shaking his head.

"Did you eat?" Rachel asked.

"Don't worry about if I ate."

Joe walked into the bedroom, reclined on the bed, and clicked on the TV. After a few minutes, Rachel came into the room, standing in the doorway. She stared at her husband who was peacefully watching TV, ignoring her presence. She was uncertain what to do, so she decided to take a shower. Maybe a cold shower would snap her out of her present condition. It couldn't hurt.

Once in the shower, Rachel turned on the cold water. The temperature was such a shock to her system when the chilly blast struck her body that she dropped her shower gel. Reaching down for the gel, she unwittingly soaked her hair. Quickly standing straight, she added some hot water. When she finally finished and came out of the bathroom, she noticed that the lights were off in the bedroom, and the TV screen was dark. It was too early for her to go to bed, so she went into the living room. There she found a blanket and her pillow sitting on the couch. Joe had put them there. *He really is mad*, she thought. Sometimes he didn't show it, and he never yelled at her, but there were signs when Joe had had enough. This was one of them. She couldn't remember when last he had done this to show his complete disapproval.

Rachel placed the pillow at one end of the couch and loosened up the blanket. Maybe she would try to go to sleep. After all, she was exhausted. Lately her energy was nonexistent, so a little extra sleep couldn't hurt. She stretched out on the sofa and pulled the blanket over her body. Right on cue, Rufus sauntered over to her and gave her a sloppy kiss. It only took one slurp to cover her whole face with his big tongue. "Nuphhht. Go way," she said, pushing at his hairy body. But Rufus didn't leave her alone. Not for hours did he seem to sleep. Periodically, he came over to where she lay, gave her a loving slurp with his tongue, and returned to his resting place. Consequently, Rachel barely slept.Rachel didn't realize that Joe wasn't actually asleep when she discovered he had placed the pillow and blanket out for her use. He had laid very still, with his back facing her, so she would think he was asleep. He did not want to talk to her then. While he knew they weren't supposed to go to bed angry, he had to take a stand. Rachel's drinking, in his mind, was out of hand. He could not abide her behavior any longer. No, he had to draw the line, and this was the time.

Around 2 a.m., a thought dawned on Rachel: *Why am I trying to sleep on the couch? We have a perfectly good guest bedroom, complete with a comfy bed. For crying out loud, I don't have to sleep here.*

Rachel got up, pillow in hand, and headed to the other bedroom. She crawled into the queen bed and pulled the covers to her neck. Rufus followed her into the bedroom. He sat at eye level, staring at her, until he decided to climb in bed with her.

"Oh, no, you don't!" she said, pushing the hairy beast off the bed. "You're not keeping me up any longer with your slobbery kisses."

Rachel woke in the morning to find Rufus sound asleep, with one front leg across her waist and his head resting on her shoulder.

TWENTY

RACHEL ENTERED her office with coffee in hand. Joe was gone when she woke up. He must have been extra quiet for her not to have heard him stirring around. After all, her sleep had been interrupted, thanks to Rufus. So coffee was in order for the day. Lots of coffee. Ignoring Loretta's warning about caffeine, Rachel knew she needed it to wake up. But she was so exhausted, it felt like her legs were dragging behind as she walked. If duty didn't call, Rachel would have gone back to bed.

There were messages on the voice mail. One said the security people would arrive earlier than arranged the day before. Earlier. Not what she wanted to hear. Searching in her desk drawer, she located the Ibuprofen. Three. It was a three pill day. It wasn't long before the security crew arrived.

"Rachel?" the man asked as he entered her office.

"Yes, and you're with Ace?" she asked, rising from her chair.

"Yes, ma'am. I already checked a little outside as I was coming in," he said. "Looks like an easy job to me."

"Oh, that's good to hear," she said, sitting back down.

"Here is what we discussed on the phone," he said, handing her papers. "Look them over and add anything if you need to."

"Okay, I will."

"So, we're going to get started now." The man nodded and left her office.

Rachel studied the contract with the accompanying paperwork. Her mind started drifting and pretty soon she was thinking about Joe. Her sweet, loving, wonderful husband. The guy who would give his life for her, no questions asked. The most devoted man she had ever met. He loved her. *Her!* Well, maybe he didn't love her so much this morning. Not after last night's performance. She had been acting drunk -– and she had felt drunk, not to mention, cross. Rachel was confused because she hadn't even had a glass of wine. And she felt embarrassed, plus remorseful. How could she make this up to Joe?

She reminisced how Joe always enjoyed a good meal. As the old saying goes: The way to a man's heart is through his stomach. That was very true for Joe. She had met him at a small café near where he was supervising a crew as they built a bank. He came in every day to the cafe for lunch. She also happened to be a regular at the café since it was near her office. Maybe not every day like Joe, but often she arrived for lunch. She had observed that Joe was always there, so they eventually noticed each other. Joe was the one to make the first move after a couple weeks of nodding and smiling.

"I see you here all the time," he had said to her as she was seated at the table. "I think we should meet."

She was pleased with the idea, and smiled, so he introduced himself.

"I'm Joe Barnes."

"Rachel Brady."

"I'm running that construction site across the street," he said, placing his hands on the back of the chair as he spoke. "This place is so convenient. Food is good, too."

"I'm around the corner at the attorney's office," she said, getting a feel for the man.

"Uh, would you mind?" he asked, lifting his hands slightly above the chair, indicating he'd like to sit down.

"No, it's fine. Please."

Joe sat across from Rachel, and their relationship began. Almost thirty years ago. Joe was twenty-six, Rachel twenty-four.

"We need to talk," Rachel said, as soon as Joe walked in the door.

She was seated at the dining room table with a glass of iced tea. Rufus did his normal rambunctious greeting of Joe.

"Okay," he said, walking to the table, giving a final pat to Rufus. "Talk."

"I acted like I had too much to drink last night, but I think I was just on a sugar high or maybe low. It was a long day; a long week. I got carried away, I ate chocolate and cookies, I don't know...," she explained with a shrug of her shoulders. She did not mention the error of entering Eneida's unit.

"Um." Joe just stared at her, waiting for more.

"I didn't like sleeping on the couch," she said, her face looking a little sad. "It was lonely. I only had Rufus, and he kept waking me up, slobbering on me. The cat avoided me. Then I went to the other bedroom."

"Um."

"What can I say? I'm sorry." She waited for him to respond.

Joe remained silent. It was clear he wasn't about to make this easy for her. Was their relationship in a crisis?

"Well, at least you didn't have to worry about me driving," she said, with a big smile on her face.

Joe didn't blink, and he certainly didn't break a smile. For sure, he saw nothing amusing or comforting in her remark. He stared blankly at her. Rachel squirmed with discomfort. This wasn't going well.

"I thought we were going to talk. Don't you have anything to say?" she asked. "Aren't you going to forgive me?"

Joe sat back in the chair and crossed his arms over his chest. "I have two words for you: stop drinking."

Rachel's face sunk to her chest. That was harsh. That was not what she had expected to hear. Joe always forgave her. What was different this time? It wasn't like she wrecked the car. Nothing that serious.

"Joe, I don't understand..."

"I know you don't. So, listen to me," he said.

Joe leaned forward and rested his forearms on the table. He looked seriously at her and began to speak.

"I love you, but I detest your behavior," he said. The words stung Rachel. "I can't stand your drinking. Now, true, you aren't drunk every night, but frequently you are. And I find that repulsive. If you think I am going to tolerate this behavior, I'm going to tell you, that's just not true."

Rachel slouched down in the chair with her arms crossed over her chest, her eyes beginning to fill with tears. The words she was hearing stabbed into her heart like a thousand toothpicks being shot from a BB gun. Each word pierced a new tenderness.

"You cannot go on drinking like you're doing and expect me to remain your husband."

Rachel's face immediately squeezed into the ugly cry when she heard these words. She raised both hands to her face and sobbed into her hands.

"I know this hurts you to hear, and you must know it hurts me to say this to you. But I'm done," he said, leaning back into the chair. "I won't divorce you, that's against my religious beliefs, but I will not continue to live with you if you don't stop drinking."

Rachel realized that the situation was much worse than she had imagined. Joe was threatening to leave her. Her sweet Joe. How could this awfulness be happening to her? The anxiety was so intense from this discussion, Rachel was actually having physical pain in her chest. The tightness there was causing difficulty in breathing, with the pain even traveling around to her back. The soreness in her legs was enough for her to have run a marathon the day before.

"But Joe, I am not..."

He put up his hand to stop her. "I don't want you to say anything. I want you to think about what I've said. I want you to sleep on the couch, in the other bedroom, I don't care which. And when you've had sufficient time to think about all of this," he said, expanding his arms, "then come talk to me with your solution."

"Solution?"

"Solution. Apologies won't count. Not now."

Rachel's eyes grew large over the thought of what to do.

Joe stood up, walking to the door.

"I'm going out to eat. You don't have to cook for me," he said, closing the door behind him.

And with that, Joe was gone and Rachel was left to contemplate the worst day in her life.

TWENTY-ONE

RACHEL SPENT that evening gathering some things from the master to make her stay more comfortable in the guest bedroom. She was angry and felt like she needed time to be alone with her thoughts, more than just one or two nights. Time to sort out what was going on with her. Also, Joe needed time to miss her presence. She brought over some of her toiletries and makeup, placing them in the guest bathroom. Now she was set for a vacation from Joe, albeit, in the same apartment.

But the more she brought over, the more she thought to bring. And the angrier she became. With each trip back to the bedroom, she felt her cheeks growing increasingly from warm to hot. Her jaw was set and she felt stubbornness enveloping her. Defiance became her friend. She knew there was chocolate and cookies in the cupboards and the Cheetos bag was in the pantry. Books! She would need some books. Rachel vowed to show Joe how lonely it felt without her. Three or four nights should bring the appropriate response from him. *He will be begging me to return.*

After finally organizing everything, Rachel changed her clothes and selected a pretty nightie to wear. It didn't fit well, too big, but she chose not to change it. She sat on the guest room bed with her feet under the covers, a two liter bottle of Coke on the end table, a chocolate bar in her hand. The Cheetos and cookies rested on the other side of her hips. However, *she wasn't drinking*. Besides, who was he to disbelieve her? At that precise time, the door swung open to the bedroom.

Joe stood in the doorway. Rachel was so angry by this point, she shot him a withering look.

No words were exchanged. None were needed. Joe left the room, closing the door.

Olivia entered the laundry room and unfolded her lawn chair. She took a small block of wood that she had brought and inserted it between the door and jamb so it allowed her to peek out. Sitting in the chair, she had the perfect view of any activity that occurred at the Rogers' unit. She thought about asking Penelope to pay extra attention to her neighbors, but realized that was her normal behavior. Maybe between the two of them, they would observe suspicious activity. Something had to be done. The police were moving too slowly.

She noticed Lola exiting their unit and almost panicked when she thought the woman was coming to the laundry room. But she turned back and reentered her unit. When Lola stepped out the next time, she had her purse and sunglasses. She vanished behind the elevator doors.

When Olivia no longer could hear the elevator, she saw Marc come outside the unit and look from side to side, suggesting to Olivia that he didn't want to be seen. He walked next door to Eneida's unit and unsuccessfully tried to open the door. Obviously annoyed, Marc returned to his unit. Olivia was puzzled. Why did Marc want to enter that unit? All the evidence had been taken surrounding the murder. She imagined the Hazmat team had cleaned up the mess by now. What could he have hoped to find?

While Olivia contemplated what she had seen, the door suddenly pushed open.

"What are you doing?" Ruby asked. "That's a weird place to sit."

Olivia was caught off guard, not able to think of a logical excuse.

"You don't even have the lights on," Ruby said, flicking the switch. "Why are you sitting here in the dark?"

"I, uh, I was," Olivia stammered. "Well, if you must know, I was meditating."

Ruby gave her a suspicious look. "Meditating? In the laundry room?"

"Why not?"

"Because it's noisy in here with machines running."

"There aren't any running now, so it's quiet. Very quiet. Until you arrived."

"Huh. What's with the wood chunk?" Ruby was looking at the block of wood on the floor, now pushed to the side of the door.

"I needed a little bit of light."

"I see." It was obvious that Ruby didn't see at all, nor did she believe Olivia. "Whatever. I came to get my laundry."

"Oh, well, let me get out of your way," Olivia said, rising quickly and folding the chair in a smooth motion. While Ruby busied herself piling clean clothes into a basket, Olivia retrieved the wood from the floor and hastily opened the door. "Bye, Ruby."

"Yeah, bye." As she escaped from the laundry room, Olivia saw the old woman shaking her head.

Rachel sat behind her desk, sipping water, and thinking about her current marital situation, when Detective France entered through the door. He nodded at her.

"Good morning," he said with a large smile. "Hope you're doing well."

"Not as well as you seem. You're more chipper this morning than usual," Rachel said.

"Umm, that could be," he answered, still smiling.

"Okay, want to share? I'm curious," Rachel pushed. "Or nosey, whichever."

"Well, since you asked," he started, "my wife and I are pregnant." He flopped down in the chair, looking very satisfied with his news.

"Really? Wow! That's wonderful news," she said, with a little smile. Rachel remembered those early days in a marriage. Pregnancy was a biggy. Those times were so exciting, filled with hope and happiness. "I am very happy for you."

"We're pretty much jumping out of our skins. It's our first." He couldn't contain his smile.

"And how far along are you?"

"Right about eight weeks," he replied. "And, no, we don't want to know what it is."

"Darn!"

The detective laughed. "We get that reaction every time."

"That's wonderful news, but it's not why you're here." She raised her eyebrows in curiosity.

"Okay, down to business," he said. "What we've discovered so far is this: Your friend knew her attacker, and let him or her in willingly, whether she buzzed the person in by the front door or opened her apartment door to a neighbor."

"Yes, we've already established that," Rachel said, waiting for some information she didn't know.

"Yes, we did, pretty much."

"Did you talk with Marc?" she asked.

"Yes, I sat down with him after he bonded out for abusing his wife."

"How did that go?"

France shrugged. "Hard to say. He didn't claim to have any real relationship with Eneida. They'd see each other in the hall, in the laundry. He knew who she was. He had heard she'd been murdered. It was all pretty loose."

"But, could he be a suspect?" Rachel wasn't liking what she was hearing. When were they going to find the monster who took her friend's life?

"There is nothing solid to point toward him," France said. "He appeared relaxed enough, considering he was being grilled. He was believable."

"Well, where was he when the murder occurred?"

"At home. In bed, probably. The time of death is an approximate."

"He didn't hear *anything*? Eneida's apartment was a mess, like maybe she put up a fight," Rachel said. "Nothing?"

"Not a sound."

"And, of course, his wife says he was with her," she said.

"Absolutely."

"Right." Rachel was frustrated. "So, where does that leave the case? In limbo?"

"Unless new evidence is found, the case is at a dead end," France said. "I don't like having to say that. News of this sort always irritates people. But we have no suspects, no leads."

"What about Jorge at the shelter? Did you talk to him?" she asked.

"He was very helpful in telling me about Eneida and the shelter," France answered. "He seemed like a decent sort, caring. An animal lover." He shrugged. "Not a killer."

"No, he isn't," Rachel agreed. "But couldn't he give you any ideas of anyone who could have committed murder on his boss?"

"Nothing. He didn't know her personal life."

"Of course not. I didn't even know much about her personal life, so I have discovered. And I was a close friend." Rachel rested her head back on her chair, looking at the detective with bewilderment. This was so discouraging to her. She wanted justice to be done, a killer found. Why couldn't the police find the murderer?

Lowering his head, France stood up. "I'm sorry I don't have more news to share or something hopeful."

"What about Penelope? Could she have heard something?" she suddenly thought to ask. "Did you talk to her?"

"She was one of the first. She didn't hear anything," he said, motioning with his hands pointing at his head. "Hearing aids, you know."

"Of course. She didn't have them in," said Rachel. "World War III is going on two doors down, and she has no clue."

"I'll let you know if something turns up, but at this point, I'm not hopeful," France said, moving toward the door.

"But what about that mystery man, the one in the coat and hat? Maybe he's the killer?"

"We have zero on that man. No video, no name, absolutely nothing," he answered. "The information we received was from an anonymous caller. Maybe the mystery man doesn't even exist?"

"And the visitor? You couldn't find out who that was?"

"I'm sorry."

"I understand. You can't create a killer. I'm just frustrated. But thanks for coming."

Thanks for nothing.

Rachel knew it wasn't his fault the case was at a dead end. She knew he was a good detective. It was just frustrating to not have any answers. Returning back to what she was doing, which was writing checks, she signed her name a dozen times. The check she wrote for the condo security system was certainly a fair price. Why no one had seen the need to install one before she became manager, Rachel didn't understand.

The door opened once again, and in stepped a woman Rachel did not know.

"Hi. You must be Rachel?" she drawled, extending her hand. "I called yesterday about renting a unit?"

The woman was very attractive, quite blonde, with shoulder length hair, and a figure that would create envy in every woman's heart. Her nails were so long, Rachel wondered how she managed to do anything, like tie a shoe lace? But she wore boots, so maybe that was never an issue?

"My name is LuAnn Riley." She had such a heavy southern drawl, it was like she was raised in the backwoods of Mississippi, rolled around in Alabama, and topped off by a walk about in Kentucky.

"So nice to meet you, LuAnn."

Rachel turned around to the key cabinet, removing the correct key to the apartment.

"I'll just show you the unit, if you'll follow me," Rachel said.

"If it's half as good as you described, I'm sure I'll take it," LuAnn said.

"The elevator is just outside those doors," Rachel said, pointing at the doors LuAnn had entered through, visible through the floor to ceiling windows that surrounded her office. "You'll use this round key to unlock the door leading to the elevator in that glass cubicle." Rachel led the way to the elevator, demonstrating what she had just said. "You'll buzz in any visitors who want to get to the elevator."

Eneida's apartment was not the one she was going to look at. It wasn't fit for viewing yet, let alone selling or renting. Rachel expected Eneida's daughter to put it up for sale, once the legalities were finished. Hazmat had done a professional clean-up within the last couple days. Rachel shuddered at the thought of cleaning up the blood on the walls and floors.

After the elevator ride, LuAnn and Rachel entered the unit that was for rent. LuAnn's mouth dropped open in appreciation of what she saw.

"Oh, I love it!"

"I thought you would."

"Oh, just a quick run through is all I really need," LuAnn said, and dashed down the hallway to the master bedroom. She returned quickly and headed over to the guest bedroom and bath.

"I really couldn't ask for more," she said, entering the kitchen. "This is absolutely perfect. It's all I need. And I love the view of the pool."

"Okay, then, let's go back downstairs and sign your lease," Rachel said. "The Chappels are great people. If you have any issues, please contact them, not me," Rachel said, placing the lease in front of

LuAnn once they were back in the office. "Their info is on the last sheet. I'll give you a copy of this."

"And I give you the check?"

"This time, yes. Next month you pay the Chappels by mail."

"I'm looking forward to moving in." Rachel noticed that LuAnn managed to sign the check, despite her claws.

"When do you expect to?"

"First thing tomorrow. I can't wait!" LuAnn was all smiles as she handed the check to Rachel.

"Welcome home." Rachel always said that to people. It made them feel good.

"If you don't mind me asking, what do you do for a living?"

"I'm a country singer, honey. Can't you tell?"

Now that LuAnn said that, yes, it fit. She resembled a younger version of Dolly Parton, complete with the big chest. And long fingernails.

TWENTY-TWO

AND SO, the girls gathered again at their favorite place, the clubhouse.

"Yes, she's really pretty, busty, southern, and has outlandishly long nails," said Rachel, sipping on a glass of iced tea. She eyed the cookies. Oatmeal today.

"Well, that is a unique addition to the community," said Olivia, also sipping.

Frowning some, Tia said, "A country singer? Well, easy come, easy go. How's she paying rent?"

"That's not my problem," Rachel said. "She rents from the Chappels. Besides, she could be doing well financially. We don't know."

"Wonder if she's made any records?" asked Olivia.

Rachel shrugged. "No idea. I haven't heard of her."

"She might have wild parties," Tia said, replacing her glass on the table. "Cause you some concern."

"So, I'll call the police," Rachel said, waving at the server. "Not my problem. Yet."

Here she was, out with the girls again. Drinking tea and eating chocolate and cookies, *shame on me*! Joe would probably be asleep anyway when she came home. She could slide into the other bedroom without him even knowing. She would only have to contend with Rufus. Besides, they weren't eating together now, not since their encounter, the big discussion. Each was pretty much living as they chose. It had been a week since the separate bedroom situation was initiated. So far, Joe wasn't missing her enough to come begging for her to return to their bedroom. *His loss*, Rachel thought.

"And so, O-liv-i-a." Rachel emphasized every syllable in her name. "How's the big romance going?"

"We are doing just fine."

"Moving in yet?"

"No. And I'm not going to." Olivia looked rather perturbed. "I already told you that I don't *want* to. Excuse me, but I have a perfect right to say no," Olivia said. "I prefer to live alone."

"How's that work if you're married?" Rachel asked.

"That's the point. We get married," Olivia said.

"What does he say about all of this?" Tia asked.

"We had a talk and he's thinking about what I said." Olivia chucked her head to the side.

"But it's too early for marriage talk. You said that yourself," Rachel said.

"Yes, but I have at least set the boundaries. If we marry, then I move in. Otherwise, I stay where I'm living," Olivia said. "He seems to understand."

Tia and Rachel exchanged looks.

"Let's change the subject," Olivia said with a wave of her hand. "I did some sleuthing today."

"Sleuthing?" Tia asked, setting her glass down.

"Yes. I was spying on the Rogers unit."

Rachel sat up a little straighter. "Well, tell us."

Olivia told the girls about her exploit earlier in the day. "And then Ruby came barging into the laundry room. Scared me to death. I didn't know what to say."

"So, what did you say?" Rachel asked, starting to grin.

"I said I was meditating."

"Meditating? In the laundry room?" Tia asked.

"That was Ruby's reaction, too," Olivia said. "It was the best explanation I could come up with."

Rachel smiled. "I'll bet Ruby didn't believe you."

"I don't think she did."

"Since when do you meditate?" Tia asked.

"I don't."

"Then why did you say that?" Tia asked.

"Because I couldn't think of anything else," Olivia said. "I couldn't say, 'I'm spying on the Rogers.'"

"I wonder what Marc wanted in Eneida's unit?" Rachel asked, looking into her glass as if she expected an answer to form.

"He's probably looking for the murder weapon," Tia said. "He did it. I know he did it."

"You shouldn't say that. We don't know for sure," Rachel said, looking at Tia. "All the evidence has been removed and the unit was cleaned, so I can't imagine what he thought he'd find in there."

"Me either," Olivia said.

When they looked back at their drinks, they realized someone was standing by the table. It was LuAnn.

"Hi, y'all!" She smiled broadly at the ladies seated at the table.

"Hey, LuAnn, join us," Rachel said.

LuAnn sat down with her mug of beer, adjusted her chair and scanned every face.

Rachel made the introductions, and the girls all greeted her.

"I saw y'all over here and I thought, oh, they won't mind if I pop over and say hi!" LuAnn gushed, smiled and acted merry. "I don't know people yet. I'm new."

"You are welcome to join us any time," Olivia said, patting her arm with her hand. "We gather to catch up a couple times a week, at least."

"Are you moved in?" Rachel asked.

"Honey, I'm officially here. And I'm so excited!" Her full lips graced the side of the mug as she sipped her brew.

"Rachel told us that you are a country singer," Tia said.

"Yes, that is my profession. I sing with a couple bands in town, so I keep pretty busy on weekends," LuAnn replied.

"Do you play guitar?" Rachel asked.

"Darlin', you wouldn't ask that if you saw my apartment. I have about twenty-five guitars hanging on the walls, my collection," LuAnn said, flexing the fingers on her right hand.

"If you don't mind me asking," Tia said, "how do you play with such long nails?"

LuAnn laughed. "People always ask me that, until I perform in front of them," she answered, flashing her nails into the air. "You see, the right hand does the strumming, so instead of a pick, I use my nails. I do minimal chords with the left hand, mostly using the length of my finger across the strings. I'm not a Keith Urban in the guitar department. My claim to fame is singing, y'all."

"But you have twenty-five guitars?" Rachel asked.

"They're different colors and designs," she explained. "I coordinate them with my outfits. Honey, it looks so sweet on stage."

All the girls nodded, like they understood.

"Do you travel a lot?" Tia asked.

"I used to, in my younger days. I still go on the road at times," LuAnn drawled. "Mostly in Florida. Otherwise, I stay in this area."

Rachel was sizing up LuAnn as she talked. She certainly was pleasant enough, pretty and vivacious. Was she Eneida's replacement at their gatherings? No one could actually replace Eneida. But maybe she was a new friend. Time would tell.

. . .

Rachel had it all planned out -- enter the apartment without causing a ruckus. She definitely did not want to wake Joe. Nor did she want to encounter another tussle on the floor with Rufus. As quietly as possible, she unlocked the door, put her keys in her pocket, opened the door, shoved the throw rug to the side with her foot, closed the door behind her, and looked around for her attacker. Nothing. So far, so good.

With a dog yummy in her hand, she ventured forth to the bedroom. Walking through the dining room and down the narrow hallway, she did not encounter any hairy beasts. What luck! Rufus must be sound asleep in Joe's room. Happy dance! She put the yummy on the counter of the vanity that separated the bathroom from the bedroom, then turned right into the bedroom. She switched on the overhead light, and was met with one woof. Rufus was waiting for her on the bed, standing in alert mode. They engaged. His eyeballs met hers. No movement. Silence. Stillness. Neither dared move. And then he pounced. Rufus leapt off the bed, flying in mid-air, until his front paws landed on her shoulders, propelling her backwards. Rufus settled on top of her, eagerly licking her face, all the while pinning her down at the shoulders with his big hairy paws.

"Murph! Noph! Ruf! O-o-o-o-ff!!"

Nothing helped, no matter what she attempted to say. Rufus was intent on slobbering his mama. Joe did not come to her rescue this time. He either didn't hear her, which was likely since she was on the opposite side of the apartment, or he just didn't choose to come to her aid. Whichever, Rachel had to do her best to disengage from her own personal Sasquatch.

After wrestling around with Rufus and trying to contain his exuberance, Rachel was finally able to crawl from under the dog. Wiping her clothes with her hands to dislodged all the hair deposited, she looked down her nose at Rufus.

"You," she said, pointing her finger at him. "You are bad."

Rufus hung his head. Rachel began to get ready for bed.

By the time she crawled into bed, Benny had joined the party. He was seated by her pillow, purring his fool head off. Rachel reached to pet him on the head.

"Such a good kitty," she cooed. "Nothing like your big hairy brother over there."

Rufus sat in the corner, casting pitiful looks in her direction.

Rachel scooted down in her bed, with Benny nary moving an inch. Once she was comfortable and dozing off, Rufus climbed onto the foot of the bed to settle in for the night.

TWENTY-THREE

RUBY CAME barreling into Rachel's office, bright and early. Rachel had barely sat down to sip her coffee.

"Well, I'm not like Penelope," Ruby sputtered.

That was certainly a true statement, Rachel thought. What was her problem so early in the morning?

"But, the noise coming from the apartment next door is not conducive to my sleep or peace and quiet." Ruby stood before Rachel, arms crossed over her bony chest, which was completely covered for a change by an uncustomary tee-shirt over shorts.

"Which one? You live in between two apartments."

"The one where that little floozy just moved in." Ruby's expression was angry.

"Floozy?" Ruby calling someone a floozy was almost comical. "Who is this person, Ruby?"

"You know, don't pretend. Probably a friend of yours, too," Ruby whined.

"You mean the attractive blond lady? I wouldn't call her a floozy," Rachel said.

"The way she struts herself around in the walkway, I think she's a floozy," Ruby said.

"Your jealousy is showing."

Ruby took a defensive stance, hands on her hips now. "I'm not jealous! What do I have to be jealous about?"

Rachel decided to direct the conversation along. "Okay, so how is she causing you a problem?"

"She plays a guitar at all hours. Even early in the morning." Ruby decided to finally sit down. "And sings. Caterwauling is more like it."

LuAnn would love to know her neighbor thought her voice sounded like caterwauling.

"Okay, I will talk to her, but," Rachel started, "she has a right to play her guitar -- and sing -- during normal hours. You'll just have to adjust to her singing."

"Why should I be the one to adjust?"

"Because she has rights as well as you. Inordinate noise is one thing, normal singing, which happens to be her career, by the way, is okay."

Ruby stared at Rachel. She could tell Ruby was thinking. Apparently, the old lady was beginning to get a little set in her ways. Ruby stood up and walked to the door, turning around briefly.

"Okay, get her to be quiet during normal evening hours, whenever you think that is," Ruby said, and walked out.

Rachel's next action was to call LuAnn. After LuAnn answered the phone, Rachel explained to her about the complaint.

"Maybe you could just restrict the times you play and sing?" Rachel suggested. "Nothing after ten o'clock; nothing before ten in the morning. How's that sound?"

"I can do that," LuAnn replied. "Honey, I didn't realize the walls were so thin that anyone could hear me."

"Another thing, you might try making nice with Ruby. She's really a dear, just a bit crusty at times."

"I've seen her in the walkway and said hi," LuAnn said. "She grunted and nodded. Darlin', she wasn't friendly at all."

"I think she's jealous of you."

"Really? Oh, my."

"Ruby is a character. You've probably guessed that already," Rachel said with a giggle.

"Well, yes, she's hard to miss," LuAnn said. "Reminds me of a madam back home."

"Don't say anything like that to her!"

"Oh, I won't, don't worry," she said. "I'll try to be extra sweet to her, win her over."

"I appreciate that," Rachel said. "Have a great day."

Now, if all of the complaints could be handled and resolved so easily, Rachel would be happy.

Joe was in the parking lot doing a bit of clean up. Kids had littered the lot last evening, so he was on self-assigned trash duty. Rachel hadn't been asking him to do any maintenance, so he was accomplishing minor jobs that were on a list for when he had spare time. As he picked up a McDonald's bag, he looked up to see the new tenant crossing the parking lot. He hadn't met the woman, but had seen the moving van unloading furniture, and caught a glimpse of her unloading a car.

"Hi, there," he called, waving his hand in greeting.

"Hi!" she responded with a smile.

Joe walked closer to her. She stopped walking to the car.

"I'm Joe Barnes," he said. "I do the maintenance around here."

"Oh, are you Rachel's husband?" she asked, giving him a big smile.

"Yes."

"Nice to meet you, honey. I'm LuAnn," she drawled.

They shook hands before LuAnn walked over to her car. Joe couldn't help but appreciate the view.

Joe continued looking around for anything that was trash. He hoped Rachel wasn't punishing him by not offering maintenance jobs. Maybe there just weren't any. But he was suspicious. This was the longest time for them to go without speaking, and they had never slept in separate rooms. Each was staying secluded in their bedrooms, only venturing into the center area when food was required. However, eating out for Joe meant he didn't frequent that area of the apartment at all.

Bundling up the large plastic bag, Joe felt sad. He missed his wife, her smile, her humor, her sarcasm. He prayed every night that she would see reason. Why couldn't she see there was a problem with her drinking? Why didn't she ask for help? Joe would have gladly helped her. He understood the attraction, the dependence. He had seen the drinking within his own family. Memories of the weekend binges his father used to have flashed into his thoughts. The way he smelled, like fruity garbage, when he mixed gin with fruit juices. How Rachel smelled much of the time. How his mother locked herself in the bedroom to avoid her husband. He knew what alcoholism looked like, smelled like. He had seen it up close. And he saw the same characteristics in his own wife.

TWENTY-FOUR

RACHEL WAS in her bedroom folding clothes when she heard a knock at the door. Joe asked to come in and she said yes.

Concern was on Joe's face. That was easy for her to see. "What?" she asked.

"Can we talk? Out here?" he asked motioning toward the neutral area.

"Okay." She stopped folding clothes and walked out of the bedroom.

They settled into chairs on opposite sides of the dining room table. Rachel had her hands folded in her lap and Joe was slouched in the chair. She looked at him to indicate he should start talking. After all, this was his idea.

"Okay, well. This isn't going anywhere, is it?" he asked.

Rachel sat still, not reacting.

"So, you haven't stopped drinking." Rachel shifted positions in annoyance. "You haven't asked for any help. I don't know what to do about this."

Rachel shrugged her shoulders. “I'm not drinking.”

"That's not an answer. Or a solution."

"So, I don't have any solutions," she said.

"Do you like living separate lives?"

"Not particularly, but this was your idea," she answered, cocking her head.

"I didn't think it would go on this long."

"Neither did I."

"Well, then, how can we get out of this mess? Will you stop drinking?" Joe looked at her, turning his palms upward. "That's my suggestion."

Rachel twisted her lips to the side.

"What if I don't like your suggestion?" She was being defiant, plus a little stubborn. But she had her rights, too. Besides, she knew she wasn't a drunk.

"Rachel, your husband has an issue with your drinking. It seems that would concern you. The fact that it doesn't is a real problem." Joe looked down in his lap, as if trying to find the correct words to say. "Rachel..." he said, pleading with his eyes as he looked up at her.

"Joe, I have not been drinking. I am not sneaking drinks. I have been trying to tell you that, but you are so fixated on me being a drinker that you haven't listened to me." Rachel was looking directly at him. "And I have been stubbornly resisting your attempts to control me."

"You have been belligerent. You've been swaying around like you've been drinking. Your breath betrays it. You don't even look the same." He sat there, letting his words fall around her.

"I don't know that to be true. Just because you say it, doesn't mean it accurate," she said. "I will, however, agree that I sway sometimes."

"I see the signs. I know an alcoholic when I see one," he said, leaning his elbows toward her onto the table. "You're getting skinny, too. It's a sign that you're not eating."

"How could you see 'the signs?'? Because I'm not an alcoholic," Rachel said, slapping the table with her hand. "And I'm eating all the time. I don't know why I'm getting skinny."

"They all say that. Deny, deny."

"You are not listening to me, Joe." Rachel tightened her jaw as she stared at her husband.

"I am listening to you."

"Did you hear me say that I am not drinking?"

"Yes."

"So, you don't believe me?"

"That's correct. I see the signs."

Rachel nodded her head and sighed with exasperation. "Joe, look closely at my face. You know I don't lie very well, so look real close," she said, facing her husband. "Look into my eyes. *I am not an alcoholic*. I have a problem, but it's not drinking."

"What are you talking about? What problem?"

"I've been feeling faint lately. Sometimes I get dizzy. I drink a lot of water, too. And I'm losing weight despite the fact that I'm eating like crazy." She pushed a clump of hair behind her ear, glad to see Joe actually paying attention to her words.

"I've noticed the candy wrappers and cookie boxes in the trash," he said.

"Not just sweets, Joe, everything. And I am unusually tired. All the time. But the one thing I am not is drunk," she said. "I drink iced tea when I'm with the girls at the clubhouse. Ask the bartender. Ask the girls. And I eat chocolate bars and cookies."

Joe sat back in his chair, wearing a concerned expression. "What's wrong with you?"

"I don't know."

"Have you been to the doctor?"

"No."

"Why not?"

"I don't like doctors."

"A friend of yours is a doctor."

Rachel waved her hand in a dismissive fashion. "Whatever."

"Rachel, I believe you," Joe said, leaning toward her. "Tomorrow you are making an appointment to see the doctor."

She slowly folded her arms over her chest, lifted her head, and responded, "Maybe."

LuAnn was struggling with her basket of dirty clothes as she headed to the laundry room at the end of the walkway. She knew she shouldn't have waited so long to do her wash, but moving into her new place, unpacking, socializing with neighbors, and so forth had interfered with her plans. She heard a voice call out to her as she all but dropped the basket.

"You need some help?" Marc asked as he exited his front door. "Here, you're going to drop everything."

Marc grabbed at the basket before it took a plunge, hoisting it into his arms. "You were about to lose everything down the side of the building," he said. "Something was bound to go through the railing and fall on someone's head."

"Oh, that would have been embarrassing," LuAnn replied, laughing. "Thank you for helping me."

"No problem," Marc said, walking along at a leisurely pace. "Pretty ladies shouldn't be hauling laundry around. Not when men are able to help out."

That was all of the conversation Lola could hear from inside their unit with the front door open. *Funny, he never helps me with the laundry*, she thought. *I'm no bigger than LuAnn. But am I as pretty as she?* Lola didn't think of herself as particularly pretty, and certainly not compared to LuAnn.

Lola stuck her head out the screened door, looking down to the end of the walkway. They had stopped at the entrance to the laundry room and were talking. Marc was animated. She hadn't seen him that way in quite a while. LuAnn was just standing there, taking in the compliments she was sure Marc was feeding to her. And she was smiling. Lola knew all too well how a smile could entice a man. *She had better not sink her meat hooks into my Marc!*

By now Marc had placed the basket on the floor between LuAnn and him so they could comfortably continue their discussion. Lola was fuming. What did they have to discuss? They hardly knew each other. Then Lola remembered that it had been Marc's idea to invite the new neighbor over for a drink. He included other neighbors as well, but the primary purpose was to get acquainted with LuAnn. That thought did not quell Lola's anger.

Marc reached down to grab the basket and LuAnn opened the door to the laundry room for him. Both entered. The door closed. Lola's heart skipped a beat. And then Marc came out by himself. Lola ducked back inside their unit before Marc could see her observing his public flirtation.

Rachel had almost reached the driveway leading to the shelter. Neither she nor Olivia had returned the cat carriers, so today seemed as good a time as any. This was her half day in the office, so she was free to escape to the country and visit the animals.

As she slowly coasted into the shelter area, she noticed some cars were present. *Great! Potential furbaby parents.*

Rachel parked her car and retrieved the carriers from the backseat. As she walked toward the buildings, she saw a couple leaving with a dog on a leash. The large mixed-breed wasn't being particularly cooperative as he lunged against the restraint. Evidently, he was on the younger side of adulthood, judging by his antics.

"You've got a handful!" she said as they passed.

"Yes, I think he's going to be a challenge," the man replied.

"You can handle him," the woman said. "Just needs dog obedience training."

"That will do it," Rachel agreed. "Good luck."

She saw Jorge up ahead of her.

"Hi, guy," she said. "Brought back the carriers, finally."

"I'll take them," he said, reaching for the carriers. "Thanks for doing this."

"I would have come sooner, but life got in the way," she said walking along with him.

"That can happen."

"How are you, Jorge?" Rachel watched as he replaced the carriers onto the shelves. He had been running the shelter by himself now for several months. She wondered if he ever saw anyone besides potential adopters? Did he get off the grounds much to function as a normal man?

Jorge turned around, looking down at Rachel. His expression was sad, Rachel thought. Not what she had expected.

"Okay most days; not so good others."

Rachel was concerned.

"What's wrong? Is the shelter having problems?" It would have broken Eneida's heart if the shelter had financial problems. This was her baby. The animals meant everything to her.

"Oh, the shelter is doing fine. We survive okay," he answered, looking down at his boots. "Eneida left money for maintenance and upkeep; we okay."

"So, what's wrong?"

"Me." Jorge looked her square in the face. "I miss Eneida. She's gone. I'm sad."

Rachel didn't know what to say. They had worked together, sure. She guessed they possibly were friends. But Eneida was the boss. He was an employee. Were they closer than that?

Jorge went onto speak. As he did, his body shifted from side to side. "We were together, every day. Sometimes late at night. Seven days a week," he said, punctuating the last sentence with a sigh.

"And you were friends. I can understand you would miss her being around."

"More."

"More?" What did more mean?

"I loved Eneida."

There it was. Jorge loved Eneida. Rachel hadn't seen that coming. Of course, the question now was: Did Eneida love Jorge? She never mentioned him in conversations. Actually, she never mentioned any man. Rachel didn't know if she had dated or not. It was not a subject for conversation. However, dating Jorge? The man couldn't have been making much more than minimum wage. How could he even afford to take Eneida on a date? Or had the shelter activities been their dates, bonding over the love of animals?

"I didn't know, Jorge," she said softly, sympathetically.

"Probably no one knew. I don't know if she loved me," he said. "But I loved her." He looked at the ceiling and Rachel could see his moist eyes.

"Is there anything I can do?" Rachel had no idea what that would be, but she had to ask. She felt badly for Jorge.

"No, nothing. I'm good," he said. "Like I said, some days are okay and others not."

"Jorge, if you need something, please let me know."

"I will, but I won't need anything." He attempted a half-hearted smile.

"Okay. I'm going to just look at some of the animals before I head home," Rachel said, pulling away from their conversation.

"Please. They love you." And with that, Jorge walked away from Rachel.

Poor man. Broken hearted.

TWENTY-FIVE

"I AM FLABBERGASTED," said Olivia.

"Me, too," said Tia.

Both women stared across the table at Rachel, each paused in astonishment with their drink in their hand.

"I know. I never knew her to be interested in any man, let alone Jorge," Rachel said.

"Well, he's a nice man. Kind to animals," Olivia said. "But how can he afford to take her out?" Olivia was expensively dressed in a green tailored pantsuit. Money was not an issue in her world.

"That was my thought," Rachel said.

"Maybe Eneida paid," Tia suggested. "We are in modern times. Women ask men out. Women pay. Sometimes. Certainly not me."

"Or me," Olivia seconded.

"Maybe they didn't go out," suggested Rachel. "Maybe it was a relationship of common interests? I don't know."

"He fell in love," Olivia said.

"Yes," Tia agreed, shaking her head sadly.

"Well, bottom line, he's heartbroken," Rachel said, rubbing both hands down her blue jeans- covered thighs. "I feel bad for him."

"Speaking of a love life, of which I have none, how is your relationship going at this point?" Tia asked Olivia, turning her full attention on the woman beside her. "In case you didn't know, I live vicariously through you."

"Well, it seems we might be taking a vacation together," Olivia said. "A cruise to Costa Rica. Separate cabins, of course."

"Oh, that's nice," Tia replied, reaching back to check the clip holding her long hair. "I have wanted to visit there."

"That is going to be an expensive trip if he's paying for two rooms," Rachel said.

"He can afford it," Olivia said.

"I'm glad to hear that. Olivia, I really hope this relationship works out for you," Rachel said. "You deserve to be pampered."

Rachel looked over at the bar and waved her arm. "Another, please," she called out. The bartender nodded. Right after that, a loud clap of thunder boomed. Suddenly, the clubhouse was plunged into darkness.

"Oh, great, we just lost power," Rachel moaned.

"Maybe it will come right back on," Tia suggested.

"And maybe not. You know we could be without power for hours," Olivia said.

"Not likely," Rachel said. The emergency lights flashed on to allow people to see where they were walking. "We are on a main power grid, so we'll receive power before some others."

The server made her way over to their table with Rachel's iced tea. After she turned to leave, Olivia reached out her hand to place it on Rachel's arm.

"Sweetheart, how long has it been now that you and Joe are separated?"

"Maybe four weeks. I've lost count."

"Can't you two talk this out?"

"We had a talk last night. I tried to tell him that I haven't been drinking and that I think something is wrong with me." She gave her friend a lopsided twist of her mouth.

"What did he say?" Tia asked.

"See a doctor. But I don't want to."

"Oh," the two women said in unison.

Silence dropped on the table like a blanket, smothering discussion. They sat in the dim lighting for a few minutes, saying nothing. The server returned to their table and looked questioningly at Tia and Olivia. Both waved their hands to indicate no, they did not want another drink. About that time, LuAnn came by the table.

"Hi, y'all," she said. "I was just over there with Marc and Lola. But Lola wanted to go because of the power outage, so she made Marc leave, too." LuAnn pulled out the fourth chair. She looked fantastic, dressed in a lowcut red top that complimented her blond hair well.

"So, you're friends now with Marc and Lola?" Tia asked.

"They've been so nice to me. Had me over to their unit for drinks with some other neighbors. Marc carried my laundry to the laundry room the other day," she said. "He's been very nice."

"I'll bet," Rachel said. "Watch him."

"Oh, honey, he's just being nice," LuAnn said with a dismissive wave of her hand. "Means nothing."

Olivia and Tia exchanged looks.

"So, are you playing any gigs?" Rachel asked.

"Yes, this weekend. Y'all should come." LuAnn gave them a bright smile of encouragement.

Tia and Olivia looked at each other, but said nothing. Rachel just sipped her tea without response, contemplating her return home.

Breaking the silence, Olivia asked, "Are you seeing anyone?"

"Not really. After my divorce, I've been hanging alone," LuAnn said. She raised her arm at the bartender. "But I might be getting in the mood now."

A server came over to LuAnn. "I'll have another draft, same as before."

"I really put my heart into my last marriage, so I'm taking it slow," she continued. "This business is hard on marriages."

"I can imagine," Tia said. "If you don't mind me asking, how many marriages have you had?"

LuAnn laughed. "Oh, my, it's a tad embarrassing, and a little funny. You gotta just laugh, you know?" She casually flipped her hair back from her face. "You see, y'all, everybody married young in my hometown. I was seventeen the first time around."

"That is young," Tia stated. The rest hummed agreement.

"But he got me to singing in a group, started my career. So, I went on the road. That's not good for a marriage," she said, accepting her beer from the server and taking a quick sip from her mug. "Naturally, he got bored at home, took up with some gal, and I got interested in the guitar player. Marriage over."

All three nodded as if they had been through the marriage with her.

"The guitar player and I had it good for a while, till he caught the scent of another female. Poof, he was gone. I stayed on the road, met a music manager and married him, even though he was twenty-five years older than me. But what did I know? Y'all, I was all of twenty-two by then."

LuAnn tilted the mug up, taking several swallows before resuming her tale. The rest of the girls held their breath, waiting for her to continue.

"That marriage lasted until my husband thought another young singer had prospects for fame and fortune. He represented her, traveled with the gal to get her career going. I either was on the road as a backup singer for several well-known country groups or I just sat at home, waiting for him. It didn't end well, y'all."

"I can't imagine it would have," Rachel said.

"Nope, he was a bum; took some of my money. All he wanted was money, not really me," she said. "So, I kept on traveling, like that rolling stone, always turning up somewhere new."

"So, you married again?" Olivia asked.

"Not for a lot of years. Y'all gotta understand, I was kinda scared and scarred. I did have a few boyfriends, though. All on my terms." LuAnn sighed at the end of her statement.

"But you said this last divorce really hurt you?" Tia said.

"Yes, it surely did." LuAnn held the mug between her hands as she silently reminisced.

"How did that marriage come about?" Rachel asked.

"Well, y'all know how you can swear off men? 'Don't want nothing to do with the bums, just leave me in peace. I'm good or better by myself.' And then someone pops up unexpected?" She set the mug back down. "Well, that's what happened. He was a charmer, sweet, handsome, and I really fell hard for that country boy. We got married in six months. And this looked like a keeper, too. Honey, we traveled all over together as a duo, both playing guitars and singing."

"That sounds good," Olivia said.

"Yes, it really was. We were a bonded couple, no competition between us, no other people tempting us. It was perfection on the road." LuAnn tilted her head down for a few seconds, gathering herself. Apparently, the loss was still raw. "And we had money. It was great," she said, popping her head up again, wearing a ragged smile.

"Well, what happened?" Rachel asked.

"He wanted a family. I couldn't give him one." LuAnn shrugged. "He didn't want to adopt, and I really didn't think any agency would give us a kid anyway, not with our lifestyle. So, we continued our duo for years, then we just got tired of the road. Once we came off, we had nothing to share. Our life was on the road. We were two strangers, living in a house, doing weekend gigs. It just wasn't the same."

"What happened?" Olivia asked.

"Nothing. And everything. We led separate lives, each willingly. Finally, it seemed silly to continue to be husband and wife. There was still more life to be had, just not with each other," LuAnn said, sighing heavily and tapping her pink nails on the side of the mug. "That was almost two years ago."

The ladies remained silent after LuAnn finished her personal story, soaking in the heartbreak their new friend had shared.

Then the lights popped back on. The power outage was over, just like LuAnn's marriage.

TWENTY-SIX

RACHEL ever so quietly crept down the hallway to her bedroom. There had been no sign of Rufus when she came in. She knew at this hour Rufus would likely have given up on her coming home and retired to the bed with Joe. All clear. Smooth sailing to her bedroom. And then it happened.

Squeak, squeal!!

Rachel's foot found the only squeaky toy in the hallway. It let off a piercing protest, causing Rachel to jump and then drop her purse. Catching her breath, she leaned over to pick up her purse. And that is when his majesty decided to make his entrance. Rufus saw his wonderful mistress bent over, so, naturally, he jumped on her, placing his paws on her rear end. Down Rachel went, crashing into a fully prone position.

The sight of his mistress on the floor encouraged Rufus to straddle her, which he loved to do, and lick the back of her head incessantly. Rachel protested to no avail. Finally, she was able to push herself into a poor example of the cobra yoga position.

"Rufus, leave me alone," she sputtered. "Get back, get off, get *something*!"

Rufus finally got the message and stepped away, looking sadly at her. Rachel bent her knees and was finally able to stand from there. Glaring down at the dog, she turned quickly, felt faint, and threw herself off balance, right into the corner of the wall leading into the bedroom. Tears sprang to her eyes due to the pain of clobbering the side of her face on the hard surface. With one hand holding her cheek, Rachel dragged herself into the bedroom and sat down on the bed.

"You."

Rufus stood in front of her, looking pathetically sad.

"Why do you torture me?"

The dog sadly eyed his mistress, raising one paw.

Rachel had had all she wanted from the day, so she rolled onto her back and went to sleep without bothering to change her clothes.

Joe was having a leisurely morning, drinking coffee and reading the newspaper at the dining room table. Rachel came gingerly walking down the hallway, obviously still half asleep. Without saying a word, she went into the kitchen for some coffee. When she returned, she noticed that Joe had a peculiar look on his face.

"What? You don't want me to sit here?"

"I don't care," he said, looking over top the newspaper.

"Then why are you looking funny at me?" Rachel pulled out the chair and sat.

"I'm not sure I should tell you. It doesn't sound like you're in a good mood."

Rachel rolled her eyes. "What's wrong? My hair's a mess?"

"What's the other guy look like?" he asked, lowering the newspaper and smoothing it over the table with his hands.

"What are you talking about? What guy?"

"The one you got into a fight with," Joe said, casually flipping his paper over one page.

"Fight? I haven't been in a fight. You're crazy." Rachel sipped her coffee from the mug between her hands, her elbows resting on the table.

Rachel remembered last night she'd had a tussle with Rufus -- again. Then she'd passed out in bed. Why was he talking about a fight?

"Did you brush your teeth yet?" he asked.

"No."

"Then you haven't looked in the mirror?"

"No."

"Maybe you should," Joe suggested.

Giving Joe an expression of confusion, she placed her mug on the table and rose to look at herself in the mirror by the front door.

"Oh, my gosh!"

Joe calmly wore a look of satisfaction as he waited for her to return to the table.

Standing in front of him, she declared the obvious, loudly, "I have a black eye!"

"You sure do."

"And I think that eye is shutting. I wondered why things looked a bit askew from this side."

"Um huh."

Rachel glared at Joe. He looked up at her, thinking better of making any further comments. Lowering his eyes, he busied himself by turning the pages of the newspaper.

"Well, I can't go to work looking like this." She sat at the table again and began sipping coffee. "For your information, this is all your fault."

Joe looked across the table at Rachel, eyebrows raised. "Pardon me? How is your black eye my fault? I didn't punch you. I haven't even seen you since last afternoon." He tossed one section of the paper onto the floor.

"That, that stupid dog of yours, Rufus. He attacked me. He pushed me into the wall last night."

"I seriously doubt that."

"You haven't trained him," she sputtered. "Rufus is unmanageable."

Rufus, hearing his name, decided to enter the room.

"You," she said, pointing at him, "you are a menace!"

"Aw, poor Rufus," Joe said, pulling the dog toward him for a hug. "Mama doesn't love you anymore."

"Ugh! You two belong together."

Rachel stomped from the room, down the hallway toward the sink. First, she would brush her teeth, cleanse her face, and then figure out how to camouflage the black eye.

TWENTY-SEVEN

WAS this an unusually busy day at the office, or was it simply her imagination? It wasn't even near the date for payment of condo fees, so why were so many people coming in and out? Everyone had looked at her with a squirrely expression on their face, probably afraid to ask why she was wearing sunglasses.

Well, gee, I couldn't cover up my black eye is why. It's morphed into a monstrous purple and blue canvas of pain.

She had purposely worn red lipstick to distract from the obvious. So far, that wasn't working well. The bruising was inching down past the rim of the glasses. Every hour it seemed to grow. If they saw her face sans the glasses, they'd probably think Joe had decked her. That would be unfair to Joe. It really wasn't his fault, even though earlier she had blamed him for her black eye.

And then Ruby waltzed into the office. "Whatcha doing wearing sunglasses here in the office?" were her first words. After a second take, she just couldn't help herself. "Lord, child, did your man hit you? Sunglasses always mean you're covering a black eye."

"No, Ruby, Joe didn't..."

"Now, you come to mama, I'll take care of you, sugar," and the next thing each knew, Ruby was hugging Rachel.

"Stop! It's okay, Ruby, really it is," Rachel said in defense of the unwanted affection. She tried to wriggle out of the embrace.

"Woman, you have a black eye." Ruby had declared the obvious.

"Thanks for reminding me."

"How'd you get a black eye?" Ruby stood back with her hands on her skinny hips. "They just don't fall down from the overhead lighting."

"Ruby, sit in that chair and calm down," Rachel pleaded in exasperation.

Ruby sat across from Rachel, waiting for an explanation.

"It's really very simple," Rachel tried to explain, knowing her explanation would probably be communicated all over the building. "The dog tripped me. I fell into the wall. End of story."

Ruby sat staring at her. "Joe wasn't involved?"

"He was not involved. He was asleep."

Silence, as Ruby contemplated the explanation. That should suffice for Ruby, as well as the entire complex, Rachel figured.

"Okay, I accept that. But I know men can be so mean."

"You know Joe, and he is not mean."

"That's true." Ruby had to agree with that statement.

"He would never hurt me. He loves me," Rachel said, pushing the glasses closer to her face.

Ruby looked at her with soulful eyes. "I'm sorry. I didn't mean any disrespect to Joe."

"I know you didn't. It's all right."

"Okay, I'll leave you with your black eye," she said, standing.

"Ruby, why did you come in here?"

"I don't remember now. Ha!" Ruby laughed.

"Take care, Ruby."

"You, too."

Rachel sighed her relief as the old woman left. But there was only a short reprieve. In walked Loretta, predictably. Usually one of them came just prior the other.

"Hello, Rachel."

"Hi, Loretta."

"You look lovely in your sunglasses. Who hit you?"

What, again?

"No one hit me." This onslaught of questions was getting on her last nerve.

"Well, dear, in my experience, women don't wear sunglasses in an office unless they are covering a black eye." Loretta folded herself into the chair across from Rachel, adjusting her olive colored pantsuit. Then she fixed her eyes on Rachel's face, waiting.

How many worldly broads are going to come into my office today to interrogate me about this stupid black eye?

"Okay, you got me, Loretta," Rachel said. "I got mugged."

"No, you didn't. I want the truth." By now, Loretta was boring holes into Rachel. Obviously, the woman was not relenting until she knew the truth.

Rachel sank back into her chair with a sigh. She felt comfortable talking to Loretta.

"I was out with the girls. You know them, Olivia and Tia. Then LuAnn joined us. When it was time to leave, I stood and felt a rush of dizziness," she admitted. "Really dizzy, maybe faint, I don't know..."

"Then what happened?" This probably was a mild admission compared to other confessions Loretta had heard over the years.

"I went home. Rufus attacked me..."

"Who is Rufus?"

"Oh, no one human. Rufus is our dog."

"Oh, okay, go on."

"He has a tendency to sneak up on me when I come home late and cause a problem for me," she said. "Like jumping on me and I fall. Slobbering all over me after and just causing me grief. But I do love the mutt."

"Of course. And I'm guessing he did the usual."

"Yeah, he came behind me after I stepped on his squeaky toy. I dropped my purse, bent over to get it, and wham! He pounced on me and I went down. When I got back up, I turned too quickly, felt faint, and hit the wall. I didn't even know I had a black eye until Joe noticed this morning." Rachel shrugged and rolled her eyes.

"Darling, how often do you go out with the girls for drinks?" Loretta folded her hands over her purse as she settled in for the discussion.

"Maybe two times or three a week. But I only drink iced tea. And eat chocolate. And cookies." She smiled to indicate she was behaving herself, not drinking alcohol as Loretta was probably insinuating.

"Well, aren't you a good girl. What does Joe have to say about that? You're not home with him during those nights." Loretta raised her eyebrows.

"No, I'm not." Rachel didn't feel she could lie to Loretta. Speaking with her was sort of like talking to a lie detector. She had heard it all, seen it all, and no doubt could smell a lie.

"And he doesn't object?"

"Well..." Rachel looked at the ceiling before answering. She knew Loretta was a person she could talk to without fear of every word being transported to absolutely every human being in the entire condo. "Yes, he objects. He's rather peeved at me currently. As a matter of fact, we're sleeping in separate bedrooms."

"That is not good."

"I know. It's been probably a month this way, maybe longer."

Loretta nodded her head in understanding, silently waiting for more.

"It all started when he asked me to stop drinking. He thought I was coming home drunk, but all I ever had was iced tea, nothing alcoholic. So, I felt rebellious, like, how dare you tell me what to do?" Rachel uncrossed and crossed her legs, getting comfortable.

"Go on," said Loretta.

"After we'd been sleeping separately for a bit, he talked with me about how I'm liking this arrangement. Believe me, neither one of us is liking it at all." Rachel shook her head for emphasis.

"Of course not."

"Then we had this talk a couple nights ago. He asked me again to quit drinking," Rachel said, scratching her head. "So, I explained to him that I wasn't drinking, but he still didn't believe me."

"So, you felt misunderstood?"

"Yes. I tried to explain to him what's been happening to me."

"What has been happening to you? Tell me."

"Well, I get dizzy when I stand, and sometimes I feel faint. I have also been eating everything in sight and drinking a lot of water." She paused to take a breath. "I've been craving chocolate and I'm eating it like crazy. It has become an addiction, lately. Apparently I act drunk to him, but I'm not, Loretta. Honest."

"That chocolate will make you fat, Rachel."

"Loretta, I'm losing weight, not gaining."

Silence enveloped the room. Each contemplated what had been said for a few moments.

Finally, Loretta spoke. "Are you thirsty?"

"Yes. I'm thirsty. All the time. And I've been drinking iced tea a lot."

"With sugar?"

"Oh, of course. Lots of sugar."

Loretta leaned forward and fixed her eyes squarely on Rachel's face. "When was the last time you saw a doctor?"

"I have no idea."

"Why don't you go to a doctor and find out what's wrong with you?"

"I hate doctors."

"That is not a good reason to avoid regular checkups." Loretta gave her a stern look. "There is no telling what is wrong with you, except one thing is very clear to me: there is definitely something going on in your body."

Rachel hung her head.

“Rachel?”

She raised her head and looked at the older woman. “Yes?”

“Go to the doctor.”

“Yes, ma’am.”

“Don’t give me that. *Go* to the doctor.”

“Okay. I will. Promise.”

"I'm going to tell you a story, Rachel. I want you to listen to me carefully, okay?"

"Okay." Rachel squirmed in her chair.

"I was injured in the line of duty, which forced me into an early retirement. After I left the police force, I felt like my life had ended. I was so wrapped up in solving cases -- and I was always the one they assigned the toughest cases -- that I felt a void, a giant hole in my life. I wasn’t married, didn’t have children, it was just me.” Loretta sighed, leaning back in her chair.

“I had to create a new world for myself. And it was very difficult. I was used to a regimented life of order and rules. Suddenly, I had so much free time, I didn’t know what to do with myself.”

“I can see that would be difficult.”

“But I didn’t give up. Eventually, I became a consultant for other agencies and began teaching courses at a college. Life went on. But one important factor helped me get there.”

“What was that?”

“I started going to church. Regularly. Never missed a Sunday if I could help it," Loretta said. "That experience helped put my life back together.”

“That’s nice.”

“It was more than nice. I started attending Bible studies and learned about the value of the Word. It was amazing how I began to feel a fullness inside.”

Rachel kept nodding her head in agreement, although she didn’t really understand what the older woman was talking about.

“When was the last time you went to church?"

"What?" Rachel was surprised by the question. Church was the last thing on her mind. Yes, Joe attended, but she rarely went with him. "I don't go to church. Joe does."

"I know Joe attends. I've seen him in church."

"You go to the same church?"

"Yes. Often we sit together."

"Oh." Rachel was learning all kinds of things today.

"I'm not a proselytizer, but church would do you a world of good. And that's all I'm going to say on the matter," Loretta said, standing to leave. "Think about what I've said. Please."

Rachel sat quietly in her chair, with her mouth slightly open. She couldn't think of anything to say to Loretta before she was out the door with a parting reminder to go to the doctor. Opening the desk drawer, Rachel pulled out a fan and began to gyrate air into her face. She was so hot. And thirsty.

TWENTY-EIGHT

THAT EVENING, Detective France paid an unexpected visit to Rachel's condo unit. Joe answered the door, because Rachel was in her portion of the condo. She came walking down the hallway after Joe called her.

She stretched out her hand to the man. "Hi, Detective. I'm surprised to see you here."

"I don't mean to interrupt your evening, but I need to speak with you. Both of you."

"Right this way," Joe said, motioning to the living room. He sat independently in a chair, while the detective and Rachel sat on the couch.

"This is probably sounding like old news to you by now. Not a lot has occurred in your case recently. We've been watching the victim's animal shelter for any clues as to who might have killed her. Recently, some news came to our attention."

"Well, let's hear it. That's great," Joe said.

Rachel nodded her head in agreement.

"We have come to learn that the manager there, and now owner according to the victim's wishes, at one time had been having a relationship with the victim, dating. They weren't just employer and employee."

"Yes, I knew that. Jorge told me he had had feelings for Eneida," Rachel said.

"You knew that? I didn't know," Joe said.

"I probably told you and you forgot," Rachel said.

"I don't think so. I would have remembered," Joe countered.

"Well, whatever, I knew." Rachel wasn't going to argue in front of the detective.

"That's interesting that you knew, that he told you himself," said Detective France.

"Why? Jorge is a very nice man. He's so kind."

"A person kind to animals isn't necessarily kind to people," Joe said.

Rachel glanced over at him and ignored the comment.

"Don't tell me you suspect Jorge?" Rachel asked. "That's just insane."

"We don't have enough information to accuse him of anything. At least not at this time," France said. "That's why I'm here. Do you know of anything in his past? Any tendency toward an anger problem? Any suspicious behavior?"

"No, not a thing. He's always been very kind and gentle. And I don't know anything about his past," Rachel said.

"Me either, nothing," Joe said.

"Well, someone killed this woman. We need to find out who, and there are no leads," France said.

"I really don't think Jorge should be a suspect," Rachel said. "I just can't see that."

"We have to look at all the possibilities," the detective said, standing to leave.

"I understand, but it's not him," Rachel firmly said. "I can't believe it's him."

"Please keep us informed," Joe said as he escorted the detective toward the door.

"Of course."

Joe turned around after closing the door, walking back toward the living room.

"Why didn't you tell me Jorge and Eneida were an item?"

"If I didn't tell you, I probably didn't think it was important enough to mention."

"I think it's important," he said, still standing.

"Well, I didn't know you would." What else could she say?

"Someone killed that poor woman, and in our condo."

"You want to pin it on an innocent man so justice is served?" She turned both hands upward, showing a lack of understanding.

"I didn't say that."

"That's what I heard."

"Then maybe you need to get your hearing checked."

"Okay, I think I'm done here," Rachel said, rising from the couch. "Going to my room now, not listening to anything else."

Rachel passed in front of Joe, close enough for him to smell her fruity body odor.

"Rachel, I'm sorry." He really looked sorry. It was unlike Joe to be nasty.

"Okay."

She kept walking until she reached the hallway, then turned back to face him.

"We need to clear this mess up between us. It's affecting everything."

"I agree." Joe had been doing his best to convince her to go to the doctor. But that decision ultimately rested on Rachel.

"Take me to church Sunday." It was a flat statement, but it had all the earmarks of being a turning point.

"Okay. I leave at 9:15."

"I'll be ready." Rachel turned and walked back to her bedroom. Joe was rooted to the floor with amazement. What had just happened?

. . .

The girls piled into Olivia's car with a mission in mind. They wanted to see LuAnn perform at the Gray Goat Saloon. They had been promising to attend one of her gigs, and now seemed like the perfect time to go. The location was somewhat near Main Street where all the bikers hung out every year around Bike Week, a highly popular event that drew thousands from all over the United States. All the blocks around Main Street were party central for sure. Once at the saloon, they parked the car and lined up outside the Gray Goat.

"I am the designated driver, okay?" Olivia announced. "I won't drink anything. I don't want my girls to get hurt."

"I'm not drinking, either, so I'm your alternate," Rachel said.

"Not a problem for me," Tia said. "I don't have to drink."

They entered the saloon, which was a bit smoky. And it was loud, ear splitting noisy. Rachel motioned for the girls to follow her because they would never have heard her if she'd attempted to speak. They found a table against the wall. Anything close to the stage was already filled. When the server came to the table, Rachel pointed to a woman close by who appeared to have a glass of soda and put up three fingers. She nodded her understanding.

By the time the server returned, LuAnn was walking on stage to sing. The girls thought she looked like a country star, dressed in white jeans torn at the knees, with a low-cut turquoise top. Lots of turquoise jewelry adorned her neck and fingers, and hoop earrings hung from her ears. LuAnn's hair was bushed out more than usual, and her makeup was heavier. Their friend, gorgeous to behold.

"That's our girl!" hollered Rachel.

Then LuAnn began to sing, strumming a beautiful turquoise guitar, obviously from her collection. The girls looked at each other with eyes wide. Their mouths dropped open, too. LuAnn could really *sing!*

They loved every minute of LuAnn's set, gaining a new appreciation of her talent and their friend. But the surprises weren't over. LuAnn carefully replaced her turquoise guitar in the standup holder and stepped down from the stage, being assisted by a man from the audience. And that man was none other than Marc Rogers.

"That slime ball!" Rachel said. She could finally be heard after the band went on break.

Olivia looked shocked and was speechless.

"Why am I not surprised?" Tia asked.

"He's disgusting. But what's LuAnn up to?" Rachel asked.

"Oh, my, I hope she's not dating him," Olivia said, finally getting her voice. "Maybe it's innocent on her part?"

Both women looked at Olivia as if she were wearing a tiara. She always saw the positive in situations. Sometimes she was just too naïve.

"Should we let her know we're here?" Tia asked.

"We should, so she knows we came to see her," Olivia said.

"And then Marc will also know we're here," Rachel said. "Do we want that? Do we care?"

The decision was out of their hands. The couple walked nearby, toward the bar. To not have said something to LuAnn would have been rude. As for Marc, well, he'd just have to take his lumps.

"LuAnn, our girl!" called Rachel, waving her arm and half standing.

LuAnn turned around and broke into an instant joyous expression.

"Ladies! You came. I'm so happy to see you." LuAnn shuffled between people in her platform boots toward their table. She hugged Rachel first since she was closest and standing now. Next came Tia, followed by the designated driver.

"I thought y'all were never gonna come see me. You've made me so happy." LuAnn was all but jumping up and down.

"We promised you we'd come. And here we are," Rachel said, spreading her arms wide.

Marc stayed around the bar, not venturing forward. Maybe he thought his presence hadn't been noticed?

"Can I sit with you?" LuAnn asked.

"Of course!" they said in unison.

LuAnn slid into a chair. at.

"Not to be rude, LuAnn, but what's that jerk doing here with you?" asked Rachel, hooking her thumb in Marc's direction.

"Oh, him? Marc? Sugar, don't be silly," she said. "He's just a good ole boy hanging around like flies to honey. I have them everywhere I go. Can't get rid of them."

The girls looked over at Olivia. Apparently, she'd been right. Innocent. At least on LuAnn's part. Marc? Not likely.

"We love your outfit, and jewelry," Tia said.

"Yes, you look so pretty," Olivia gushed.

"Ditto. You're amazing, LuAnn. I love your voice," Rachel said.

"Oh, now y'all have gone and embarrassed me," LuAnn said. "I'm just me doing my thing, that's all."

"And she's modest," Rachel remarked.

They all laughed.

The server came by, asking LuAnn if she wanted something from the bar.

"No, honey, I have my bottled water on stage. But thank you."

The other ladies ordered another round of soda. LuAnn returned to the stage for another set, which the girls remained for. Marc disappeared somewhere, not that they cared. The girls were just relieved that LuAnn wasn't running around with a married man. All in all, it was a great night. And they arrived back home safely. Rachel even made it to her bedroom without incident.

TWENTY-NINE

THE ALARM RANG true to the setting of the timer. It had a clanging sound that she found highly annoying. Rachel groaned as she rolled over in the bed. Sitting on the side of it, she reminded herself she was rising early on a Sunday morning to attend church with Joe. It wasn't a first, but it was significant. It had been her suggestion, after all.

She had showered the night before, so she was good to go. After brushing her teeth, she padded into the kitchen in her soft slippers. Joe had already made coffee. What a guy! She poured a cup for herself, adding the necessary sugar and creamer. She could hear Joe in the shower, so she returned to her area to get ready, cup in hand.

About an hour later, Rachel was waiting at the door. She'd already eaten a boiled egg, had her coffee, so she was ready for whatever was in store for her on this Sunday morning. Joe emerged, nicely dressed in slacks and a good shirt. This was Florida, no one dressed up for church. Joe was actually better dressed than most who would show up, considering they normally appeared in jeans and tee-shirts. Maybe even shorts. Probably the pastor would be the best dressed in the crowd, but even ministers in many churches were more casual than what Rachel remembered from her youth.

"Morning," Joe said when he saw her. "You look very nice."

Rachel didn't plan to be one of the more casual people in church. After all, she did have respect for the church, and had made some effort to put on a pink dress and heels. Okay, they were sandals, but they had a heel. She knew she looked like she was going to church. And she wanted to impress Joe with her effort. This was important. She wasn't sure why, but today mattered.

"Thank you. You look nice, too."

They were both in a highly agreeable mood. Each wanted to please the other. Their banter while driving to church was casual and friendly. When Joe mentioned to the pastor as they entered that his wife was attending today, the pastor was very kind toward her. But not pushy. Rachel appreciated that.

It wasn't long after they sat down that Loretta came down the aisle. Both Rachel and Joe motioned for her to sit with them, but she waved her hand to decline. Loretta probably recognized that they needed to sit alone as husband and wife.

Rachel didn't know what to expect from the service. She remembered from her childhood the heavy hymns accompanied by organ music, the readings, and a loud sermon being delivered. But she had not attended this particular church with Joe. He had always brought her to the traditional service in other churches. Evidently, he had thought better of that approach, telling her this was the contemporary service, and it was different from what she had experienced in the past. He had indicated that he thought she would really like it.

The music burst forth, with drums, guitars, and a keyboard. Approximately ten men and women stood on the platform performing music or singing. She was amazed over what she heard. This was not like any church she remembered. The music was upbeat and moving, making her want to sway. This service was exciting. It brought chills to her arms, and widened her eyes in surprise. She began to clap. Rachel moved her body with the rhythm when standing. Glancing at Joe, she smiled her appreciation.

When it came time for the sermon, there wasn't any hellfire and brimstone. Rather, it was uplifting and had a positive message. She was encouraged to pray and seek direction from the Holy Spirit. The Bible was stressed as holding answers and how she could experience the Word in general to lead her. Nothing upset her or made her feel uncomfortable. She smiled at Joe. She smiled, period. She was happy to be in this place of worship.

Joe and Rachel left the church and drove home. The entire time, Rachel felt like her body was singing praises. And she kept smiling. She felt *so happy*. Never had she felt like this after attending church. What had happened? She didn't know. All she knew was that she was happy.

On Monday morning, Marc Rogers walked into Rachel's office.

"I have the association fee," he said, placing a check on her desk.

"Have a seat, Marc, I'd like to talk to you." She motioned to the chair in front of the desk. He looked fidgety as he sat.

Rachel folded her hands in front and relaxed her arms across the desk. This was the perfect opportunity to ask him about something that was bothering her.

"I have a question for you, Marc," she said, her eyes piercing his. "Someone saw you trying to go inside Eneida's old apartment. What did you hope to find?"

For a split second, Marc looked like a kid who just got caught stealing candy in a store. Regaining his composure, he tried to deny the incident. "I don't know what you're talking about."

"Not buying it, Marc. You were seen by someone I trust." Rachel was not letting this man get away with anything. She wasn't the police, so she didn't have to be polite or respectful of his rights.

Marc scratched the back of his neck, buying time. Finally, he spoke. "It was dumb. Sheesh. I thought maybe I could find her diary," he said, shaking his head and rolling his eyes.

"Her diary? How did you know she had a diary?" Even Rachel didn't know her friend had a diary.

"I saw it one time when I was over," he said. "It was just sitting there on the table. The word 'Diary' was on the front cover."

"What were you doing at Eneida's unit? Was Lola with you?"

"Nah, she didn't come."

"Yet you were there alone?" This was the visitor the daughter had mentioned, the unwelcome one.

"Um, yeah. Just me." Marc shrugged. "So what?"

"Why were you there?"

"Uh, I kinda liked her," he said, nervously running one hand through his hair.

"You're a married man, Marc. Don't you think it was inappropriate to be visiting a single woman, alone?" Rachel was doing her best not to call him names.

"Uh, well, maybe."

Rachel frowned at him. "Maybe? How about maybe you shouldn't have been there?"

"I guess." He shrugged again.

"Why did you want her diary? What did it contain you didn't want anyone to see?"

"That I was visiting her."

"How do you know the diary had any indication of your visits?"

"I didn't," he said. "But if it did, I didn't want Lola to learn about it."

That was a plausible answer. But was it the truth?

"I see. So, if you'd found the diary, what would you have done with it?" she asked.

"Throw it in the incinerator, of course." He kind of smiled over that idea.

Rachel sat back in her chair, her gaze blazing through Marc. She shook her head slowly.

"Did you kill Eneida?" *Hey, why not just get the question out there?*

Marc looked stunned at the question. "No!"

"Come on, Marc. Did you kill Eneida?"

"No way! It wasn't me." His expression looked honest. But some people are good actors.

"Okay, I believe you." Rachel didn't really believe him, but she wasn't about to tell him. "I'm done asking questions. You can leave now."

Marc stood on his slim legs, attempting to look casual as he walked out the office towards the parking lot. As soon as Marc had driven away, Rachel got a key from the key box and headed to the elevator. When she reached the eighth floor, she went directly to Eneida's old apartment. Taking a quick breath, she unlocked the door and walked into the former murder scene.

THIRTY

SHE REMEMBERED the blood on the walls, the broken glass, none of which were present now. Telltale black dust remained on the furniture where the forensic people had sought fingerprints. A large portion of carpet had been pulled up and removed, and a section of wall where the fan of dripping blood had once been also was removed. She suspected Margarita was going to abandon the property since she had not made any effort toward fixing up the unit for sale or claimed any of her mother's belongings. *Too depressing.*

Rachel stood in the center of the living room. "What happened, Eneida? Who killed you?"

She walked around, not sure where to begin looking for Eneida's diary. Rachel walked into the bedroom, the one she knew Eneida used. Nothing looked out of place in there, just a typical bedroom that obviously belonged to a woman. All the accoutrements screamed female. She skimmed her eyes around the room, looking for anything. There had to be a clue. However, wouldn't the police have found any valid evidence? They hadn't allowed access to the unit for two weeks. Surely, they had found everything of importance. If the diary had been in plain sight on the table, they would have confiscated it. Even if the police did have the diary, Detective France was not obligated to tell her. Maybe this was a futile search.

Crossing the living and dining areas, Rachel walked down the hallway toward the other bedroom. The room appeared pristine, as did the bathroom and counter area. Rachel thought about tearing the bed apart, but why would Eneida hide her diary in such an inconvenient place? The more likely location would be her bedroom.

She returned to Eneida's bedroom.

"Where would you hide a diary?"

Rachel entered the bedroom again. She walked over to the night stand and opened the drawer. It was empty.

"Of course."

She continued to snoop around, even going into personal drawers where Eneida's nighties and underwear were stored. Flipping through the stacks of garments, she found nothing unusual, however, she felt a bit embarrassed doing this.

"Sorry, Eneida."

What about the bed? It sat neatly put together, not giving a hint that anyone had sat down on it since the murder. Rachel moved closer to the bed, ripping down the comforter and flipping up the pillows, but nothing was underneath. She thrust her hands between the mattress and bedsprings, running them down the length of the bed, but found nothing. Around to the other side she went, and then across the foot of the bed. Still nothing found. She was about ready to give up.

"Oh, wait."

There *was* something tucked under the mattress. Her hands discovered an object pushed way up that felt like a paper bag with something inside. Sliding out the bag and contents, she sat on the foot of the bed, opening the bag. What was inside made her heart leap. It was a diary! The word was clearly embossed on the cover, just like Marc had said. Rachel closed the bag and marched out of the unit, locking it behind her. She called Detective France as soon as she returned to her office.

While waiting for the detective to come to retrieve the diary, she was greatly tempted to look through it for clues. However, she didn't want to contaminate any evidence that possibly would be on the diary. Her own fingerprints didn't need to appear on the book, either.

LuAnn entered Rachel's office with a puzzled look on her face.

"Good afternoon, LuAnn."

"Hi!"

"So, what's up? How is your gig going?" Rachel hadn't spoken with LuAnn since the girls had seen her perform at the Gray Goat Saloon.

"It's doing fine; I'm pleased."

"What about Marc? Is he still hanging around there?"

"Unfortunately, yes." LuAnn decided to sit.

"Sorry about that."

"Me, too. More so sorry for Lola," LuAnn said. "Honey, he hasn't taken the hint that I'm not interested. By now, Lola must be wondering where he is so often at night. She probably thinks he's having an affair."

"Yes, she probably does," agreed Rachel. "Maybe you should level with him."

"I tried that, but he still comes around. He says we're friends. Well, friends don't look at me like he does. Darlin', that boy has other things in mind." LuAnn shook her head in frustration. "He keeps helping me off the stage after my sets. Maybe I need to speak to the bouncer?"

"Hm, yeah, put a little fear into him."

About that time, Lola opened the office door. Her expression abruptly changed when she saw LuAnn sitting in the chair.

"Hi, Lola," Rachel said. LuAnn also gave her a greeting.

Lola turned her head to focus on Rachel, giving her a half-hearted smile.

LuAnn decided this was her cue to leave, so she stood. "Well, ladies, I have things to do," LuAnn announced. "Y'all have a great day."

"Bye, LuAnn," Rachel said. Lola remained silent.

"So, Lola, what brings you here?" Rachel asked with a smile.

"Well, it's Marc," Lola said slowly.

Rachel noticed Lola's eyes were red and appeared moist.

"I think he's having an affair -- with that woman!" Lola pointed at the door where LuAnn had just exited. "She's a home wrecker. I want her out of here."

"Lola, I can't ask her to leave because you suspect she's having an affair with your husband. That is really none of my business." Rachel motioned for Lola to sit in the chair. "Besides, do you really know he's having an affair? And why do you think it's with LuAnn?"

"Because he had matches in his pockets from some slinky bar!" Lola spouted. "I know she sings there. She told me. And he hasn't been home most nights. He won't tell me where he's been. So, I know he's having an affair with her."

Once again, Rachel felt like Dear Abby. None of this was her problem, but everyone in the condo seemed to think she held all the answers to whatever difficulties they had. But this was a tricky situation because she knew more than Lola. Even though Rachel thought Marc was a rat, she didn't feel comfortable telling Lola what she knew. Besides, they weren't having an affair, according to LuAnn. The blame was all on Marc, not LuAnn. But she couldn't say that to Lola.

"I'm sorry, Lola. I don't know what I can do to help you."

Lola looked sadly at Rachel, then her face morphed into the ugly cry. Big tears rolled down her cheeks and her shoulders shook.

"Oh, girl...is Marc worth all of this emotion?"

"Ehhhhh, yuuuuu, mumumumum," she responded.

"I can't understand a word you're saying."

Lola took a deep breath and loudly wailed, "I love him!"

Oh, brother.

She reached for some tissues and handed them across the desk to the weeping woman. Lola accepted the offer and sniffled into the tissues.

"Maybe you should go home and have a talk with Marc."

"He's at work. At least he's supposed to be," Lola said, blowing her nose.

"I'm sure he's at work. Go home. Make him a nice dinner. Have a little talk after," Rachel suggested.

Lola nodded her head as she wiped her nose. She gave an inaudible response, then stood to leave.

"Bye, Lola."

"Thnurffffoo," she responded behind the tissue as she left.

No sooner had Lola exited the office, than in walked Detective France. Rachel handed him the paper bag with the diary, and explained how she came to find it.

"I'll let you know if we find something of value," he said, taking the bag and contents.

"Yes, please do. I want to know the minute you find out."

And then he left. Alone at last.

Who could have anticipated when she and Joe had moved here that they would encounter so much drama? And a murder. Rachel needed a vacation.

THIRTY-ONE

DURING THAT EVENING, the power to the condominium went out again. Unfortunately for LuAnn, it happened when she was in the laundry room. As she bent over the dryer, pulling out her garments, the lights went out. It wasn't a well-lit area to begin with, so when the power went out, the laundry room was plunged into total darkness, much worse than when the lights went out recently in the clubhouse. There were no emergency lights in the laundry room.

"Oh, man!"

LuAnn raised up from the dryer, bumping her head on the top of the opening. She placed her hand instinctively to her head and turned around. That's when she felt a punch to her stomach. She doubled over, groaning, wondering what had happened. Then she felt something covering her, like a sheet, although she wasn't certain what it was. However, it did smell freshly washed. LuAnn's movement was cautious, and she felt pain in her sides, like someone was striking her. Confusion ensued as she continually felt blows being delivered to her body.

"Stop!" she called out.

But the assailant didn't cease, rather, kept striking her wherever the blows landed on her body and head.

And then she fell to the floor, out of breath. LuAnn felt a kick to her side and heard something fall on the cement floor. The door to the laundry room squeaked open and closed.

Fleeing the scene.

After some time had passed, LuAnn regained her composure and painfully lifted herself from the cement floor. Flailing at the covering, she was able to stand and finally release herself from whatever was holding her. That's when the lights went back on.

LuAnn looked quickly around to see who was in the laundry room with her. No one was visible. She saw a sheet lying to the side on the floor. Her sheet.

"Who's in here? Come out, you coward!" she said, knowing full well it was unlikely they would.

No sounds, no action. LuAnn again looked about from where she stood for any sign. It wasn't a large room, so she could easily see everything. But she saw no one. Obviously, they had fled. Why would anyone want to attack her? And then she saw what looked like a wooden mallet on the floor. She painfully bent down to retrieve it. The object appeared to be a wooden meat tenderizer, something found in anyone's kitchen. The weapon of choice. LuAnn stuffed it into a pillow case, flinging the case into her laundry basket and began gathering the rest of her clothes from the dryer. LuAnn felt sharp pain in her sides when she lifted the basket. Slightly confused, she left the laundry room with effort. Walking back to her unit, she kept looking down the walkway to see if anyone was around. Had anyone seen her attacker? Was the attacker still here? She didn't know, and realized she wasn't meant to know. Someone didn't like her living here. That was certain.

LuAnn was the first person to enter Rachel's office the next day.

"Honey, I was attacked last evening," she announced.

"*What*? Attacked by whom?" Rachel asked.

"I have no clue whatsoever, but someone was wielding this." LuAnn gingerly held out the wooden meat tenderizer for Rachel to see.

"That's an odd weapon," Rachel said. "Did this happen at the Grey Goat?"

"No. In our laundry room, darlin'. When the lights went out last night."

"No way! That's awful!" Rachel said. "I automatically thought it happened at your work."

"I didn't work last night," LuAnn said. "Whoever attacked me bruised my ribs with that thing, so I didn't go in."

"I'm so sorry, LuAnn," Rachel said, looking pitifully at her friend. "Did you call the police?"

"Not yet. I wanted to tell you first."

"Did you go to the doctor?"

"No. I feel better this morning, so I'm okay, honey," LuAnn said. "I'm sure it's nothing serious."

"Well...If you say so. But let me call the police from my office," Rachel said, reaching for the phone. Rachel dialed the number for the police. It didn't take long before an officer arrived.

Sgt. Bates was a formative woman, dressed in the standard green uniform. She pushed her hat back from her tanned face and pulled out a notepad and pen, obviously anxious to begin.

"I have no idea who would do such a thing to me," LuAnn said in answer to the officer's first question. "The lights went out and I couldn't see anything. Then someone put a sheet over me –one of my sheets from the dryer -- and started pummeling me with a meat tenderizer. Can you believe?"

"A meat tenderizer?" the sergeant asked.

"Yes, honey. This one," LuAnn said, sticking her arm out to show the officer the object in her hand.

"That's an odd weapon, don't you think?" Rachel said.

"Yes," the officer agreed. She reached into her back pocket for a bag to contain the evidence.

"Anyway, this person hit me a bunch of times in the ribs and landed a few blows to my head, too."

"And you do not know who did this to you?" Sgt. Bates asked again.

"No idea at all, sugar."

"Does anyone have a grudge against you in this building?" she asked, writing her notes swiftly. "Do you have any enemies here?"

"No, honey, I haven't even lived here very long."

"You're sure?"

"My one neighbor is somewhat jealous of me, but she's something like ninety-three," LuAnn said. "I don't think she's capable of assault."

"You never know. What's her name?" the officer asked.

"Ruby."

"Ruby what?"

"I don't know," LuAnn said.

"Moskowitz," Rachel answered for LuAnn. "Ruby Moskowitz. But she didn't do this."

The sergeant looked up from her pad to Rachel and back down again. It was clear she wasn't dismissing any possibilities.

"Her apartment number?" Sgt. Bates asked.

"804," Rachel answered. "What about Lola?" She looked over at LuAnn.

"Oh, yes, and then there's Lola," LuAnn remembered. "She's jealous of me. Very jealous. Her husband has been paying too much attention to me. But she doesn't know the half of it. If she did, I'd say go look her up for sure. Frankly, honey, I don't think it's either one. Lola is so meek. And Ruby is just plain old."

"Will you allow me upstairs, please? To visit these women?" the sergeant asked Rachel.

"Of course," Rachel said, rising and motioning toward the elevator. "Lola's apartment is 809. Follow me."

Rachel led the officer to the glass enclosed elevator entry, unlocked the door, and even pushed the correct button for her. After wishing the officer a good day, she returned to her office. LuAnn was still sitting in the chair.

"Ruby is going to have a hissy fit after that sergeant grills her," Rachel said.

"No doubt, honey. Maybe I shouldn't have said anything about Ruby," LuAnn said. "But she was the only one to openly act like she had a problem with me. And Lola. She only talked to you about her suspicions. She was always pretty nice to me."

"It's okay, LuAnn. This will just give Ruby something valid to complain about."

And complain she did.

As soon as the officer left, Ruby was on the phone to Rachel, screaming into the receiver.

"I had just woken from my nap, someone is banging on my door, and when I open it, there's a cop standing there." It wasn't difficult for Rachel to tell Ruby was angry.

"Oh?"

"And she wants to know if I attacked LuAnn. *Me*? I may not look it, but I'm ninety-three, for crying in the beer. I don't go around attacking people at my age. Who does that?"

"I hope not," Rachel said, barely able to get a word in.

"Who sent the cop up here?"

"I have no idea," Rachel said. She felt it was best to lie to the irate woman and let her think it was a random visit.

"Well, if you find out, give them a piece of my mind. The idea, me attacking people."

"I am so sorry, Ruby. Have a cup of tea and relax."

"It will take more than tea." Ruby hung up the phone.

Chocolate?

What she had to do to keep peace in the condominium.

THIRTY-TWO

RACHEL EASED herself into the tub of hot water. Pretty pinkish bubbles glistened as they gathered together over her body. She felt very faint and a touch confused. Overwork due to the murder had made her badly in need of a vacation. She would have to mention that to Joe. They were slowly patching their relationship, so maybe he would be amicable to a vacation. Get away from the stress caused by the murder, and the misunderstandings they had experienced; make it a second honeymoon. The lazy thoughts running though her brain made her sleepy, and so she drifted off...

Joe entered the unit, greeted happily by Rufus.

"Rachel?"

The apartment was dark since they had returned to standard time and no lights were turned on. He looked in the kitchen, but his wife wasn't there. No dinner started. Joe walked down the hall to her bedroom, but she wasn't there. As he passed through the dining room again, he noticed the car keys sitting on the table. Joe entered their bedroom, but Rachel was not there, either. Then he noticed the bathroom door was shut.

"Rachel?" he called, knocking on the door. "Rachel? Are you in there?"

Joe turned the door knob and pushed open the door. He saw his wife in the tub, her nose just hovering above the water line. He screamed her name as he jumped over to the tub in one quick motion, reaching into the water to pull out Rachel's body. He spun around, lowering her to the rug on the floor. "Rachel!"

Her head fell toward Joe, her eyes closed.

Joe shook her slightly, not totally sure what to do, then he patted her cheeks. Lowering his head to Rachel's chest, he heard her heart beating regularly and could feel her breath on the back of his neck. Joe stood, reaching for the phone in his back pocket. He dialed 911.

Sitting in the emergency waiting room for what seemed like hours, Joe was beside himself with worry. One nurse had come out to advise that Rachel was coming around. He thanked God his wife was alive and prayed for her full recovery, from what, he didn't know. And he sat miserably in his aloneness. What had happened? What was wrong with his wife?

"Mr. Barnes?" A nurse at the desk called his name. He hurriedly walked over.

"Your wife has been taken to room 224. You can go up and see her."

"Thank you," he said, and quickly found the elevator, mashing the button flat for the second floor.

Joe walked into Rachel's room and stood at the foot of the bed. She was propped up by pillows and wore an ugly hospital gown. He was amazed how pale she looked. He'd never seen anyone so pale before.

"Joe?" she said, opening her eyes.

"Rachel, I'm so glad you're all right."

"Am I? I'm not sure what happened."

"I can tell you what happened," said a voice from behind Joe. It was the doctor.

"I'm Dr. Haskell," he said, reaching his hand out to Joe. He was a tall man, slender in body, wearing the obligatory white coat. "Hello, Rachel," he said, turning his head toward her. "I am sorry to tell you that you have diabetes. You were fortunate that your husband found you."

Joe's face looked stunned, his mouth gaping a little. "Diabetes?"

"Yes. She must have been experiencing symptoms before this happened," he said, looking again at Rachel.

"Yes." Rachel nodded her head. "Dizzy, faint, thirsty, and oh so tired. Craving chocolate and all sweets, too."

Joe looked at his wife in surprise. "You knew?"

"I suspected."

"She's a Type One. We have prescribed insulin for her and a diet that she must adhere to," Dr. Haskell said. "Rachel will have to stay here while we monitor her. Once her blood sugar reaches a normal range, she can return home."

"I understand," Joe said. "Whatever it takes to get her well."

"You understand that she won't be cured? She will have to monitor her blood sugar level from now on," the doctor said.

"Yes, I understand," Joe said. "I will support her, no problem there."

"Good." And with that, the doctor left the room.

Joe joined Rachel at their dining room table three days later. It was early in the morning, earlier than usual for Rachel to be awake. She had made coffee, so Joe grabbed a cup and sat down. She gave him a little smile. He knew something was up.

"So, you look chipper this morning. Kind of early for you."

"It is, but I knew you'd be up."

"So, what gives?"

"I want you to take me to the doctor today. I have my first appointment with an endocrinologist."

Joe nodded at her. "Of course. I can do that."

"I was doing research online about my symptoms before I landed in the hospital," she said.

"Yeah? What did you find out?'

"That I might have diabetes."

"You do have diabetes."

"We know that now, but I was just suspecting at the time. All that behavior you thought was me drinking too much, it wasn't. I knew that," she said, lifting her cup to her lips and taking a sip. "So, I did my research and I found that I was showing signs of diabetes."

"That's a serious disease."

"I know." Her concern was clearly written on her face.

"What time is the appointment?

"Two o'clock."

"Okay, I have a few jobs to do, so, I'll get them out of the way and come back here to keep you company."

"Fine with me," she said, giving him a little smile.

Rufus walked over, placing his head on Rachel's lap. She stroked his head absentmindedly.

"You know I'll always support you. And I'm so sorry, you have no idea how sorry I am that I thought you were drinking when you weren't." Joe slapped his forehead with his hand. "Such a dummy!"

"You didn't know. It's okay, really," she said. "I could have made the same mistake if the situation was in reverse. I love you."

"I love you, too," he said, approaching her. Joe bent down and kissed her on the cheek. She quickly kissed his cheek as well. This was the first affection they had exchanged since the separation of bedrooms. Joe stood back, looking down at her. She was so pretty, and so vulnerable.

"It's going to be all right," he said. "You'll get through this."

Rachel smiled up at him as he stood in front of her.

"With your help, yes, I will."

Rachel sat by herself, in her thoughts, as she sipped her coffee. She had avoided the inevitable for too long when she should have put on her big girl panties and faced whatever was happening inside her body. Her avoidance of going to a doctor had been immature. But she knew Joe would help her recover now. She trusted him. She loved him. Her sweet husband, Joe. Always dependable and by her side, through thick and thin. Joe.

It was slightly after three o'clock. They were walking toward the car they had left in the parking lot before attending Rachel's first appointment with the doctor. Both were silent. Rachel was digesting the experience. Joe was looking out the corners of his eyes for signs of her reaction to what she had heard. Rachel knew it was hard for him to tell what her thoughts were.

Silence lingered between them as they entered the car and drove home.

"Well, I'm not surprised over what he said. But I would have liked to be pleasantly surprised with better news," she finally said.

"I'll help you anyway I can. I'll be there for you to talk to." Obviously, he would assist Rachel. She knew that already.

"I know."

"And you can go to church with me."

"Oh, yeah. That would be a good idea. I'm going to need a Higher Power to get me through this."

"Um huh."

"Guess I won't be sleeping in on Sundays."

"Nope."

"But, I love that church anyway," she said. "So, it's a good plan."

Rachel looked over at Joe as he pulled into their designated parking spot. She knew she was lucky to have Joe. He was a good man. Solid. God had certainly blessed her with this man.

THIRTY-THREE

IT WAS no secret what time LuAnn left for work in the evening. Anyone with eyes could watch her routine. Unfortunately for LuAnn, Lola was walking toward her on the walkway when she left on that particular evening. She was sure Lola had purposely planned this encounter. It was just too coincidental after the officer had paid her a visit.

"You!" shouted Lola, extending her arm to point at her. "Why did you send the cops to my door?"

"Honey, I don't know what you're talking about."

"Yes, you do! Did you put my husband up to calling the cops?" Lola asked.

"Lola, I have no clue what you're talking about," LuAnn said. "Why would I do such a thing? I barely know your husband."

"Oh, don't give me that. I know you want my husband. But you better keep clear of him, you loosie goosy!" Lola's face was contorted into an ugly snarl. LuAnn was alarmed by her attitude.

At this point in her life, LuAnn was tired of jealous women, and this entire situation was compounding her frustration. She had encountered them frequently in her line of work. But having received a beating recently, plus still smarting with bruised ribs, she was not in the mood for wacky women. However, she managed to muster some decorum.

"Lola, calm down..."

"Don't tell me what to do! I know your kind. You go after married men. You like them married because there's no commitment and can fly away at any time," Lola said, now pushing up the long sleeves on her yellow shirt to her elbows in an offensive posture, leaning toward LuAnn. "Well, I'm married to this man. I am committed to him. I love him. So, stay away from Marc or I'll do something you won't like."

"What, beat me up in the laundry room again?" LuAnn couldn't help it, the words spilled out.

"That wasn't me," Lola said, pulling herself up straight. "I wouldn't do something like that. And that's exactly what I told that police woman. It wasn't me."

"Really, Lola, this is so immature and not necessary. Nothing is going on between me and your husband. Absolutely nothing." LuAnn was frustrated enough not to slink quietly away. She stood her ground in front of Lola, not budging, despite the rib pain.

"I don't believe you. Women like you lie all the time. So, I'm telling you to leave Marc alone!" Lola hollered. "And don't threaten me with more cops!"

By now, all the commotion had brought a couple neighbors to their doors to see what all the fuss was about. LuAnn was embarrassed and Lola was oblivious to the attention.

"Have a good evening, Lola," LuAnn said as she walked around her. "I have to get to work."

Lola took the opportunity to push LuAnn in the back with her hand. LuAnn quickly turned around, facing Lola. She held her hand up in the air and said, "Watch it." With that warning, LuAnn walked backwards two steps, then turned around and walked away from Lola, adjusting the strap on her white top that had fallen off her shoulder. She got on the elevator without further incident.

. . .

Penelope, who had been watching the whole exchange, knew it was going to be a noisy night next door at the Rogers' unit. Lola would start screaming at Marc the moment he entered the apartment. Marc would yell back at her and then the hurling of objects would begin. Ugh, Penelope just shook her head, bracing for the racket. Even without her hearing aids in, she would hear the commotion. All night.

And Penelope wasn't wrong. When she looked over at the clock beside her bed, it was well past 2 a.m., and the feuding couple had been hurling both words and objects for hours. She imagined bouncing vases, a remote control, dishes, and books keeping her awake.

This behavior has gone on way too long.

Rising from her bed, Penelope took matters into her own hands. Before, she had always relied on Rachel to handle the disturbances, but not tonight. Penelope had had enough. She called 911 after putting her hearing aids back in and slipping a housedress over her head and slippers on her feet.

It wasn't long before she heard her buzzer go off from the main entrance. She pressed her button and heard a man say, "Police. You called?"

"Yes, unit 809. They're still at it." With that, she buzzed the police into the building. Shortly, she heard the elevator rising as she stood by her front door. Four men with large physiques exited the elevator. Penelope pointed to the next unit.

"You can hear them for yourself," she said as they marched by.

"Police, open up!" the first man called out, banging on the door with his fist.

The racket suddenly ceased and the door opened.

"Officer?" That was Marc's voice. Penelope knew it well. She'd been listening to it all night, even with her hearing aids out.

"We need to come in to see if your wife is okay," the second man said.

Penelope heard the door creek open fully. All the men entered. She walked over and stood in front of the door, listening and watching. From what she could see, the unit was in total disarray. Nothing was positioned where it should have been, and various items, too many to count, were strewn all over the room. Penelope couldn't believe what she was seeing. Then she gasped when she saw Marc scantily clad in ripped under shorts and a ratty t-shirt. He had a smear of blood on his face, what appeared to be a gash at his thigh below the torn shorts, and blood seeping out at his torso. He was covering the wound with his left hand, or maybe trying to stop the bleeding.

"Mrs. Rogers? Come out here," demanded one of the officers.

When Lola came out of the bedroom, Penelope gasped again. The woman's nightie was torn at the shoulder, and there was blood smeared on the front. But what was most alarming was the knife Lola held in her hand – plus the scary expression she wore on her face. The old woman thought Lola looked deranged.

"Put the knife down," commanded one of the officers.

Lola let the knife slide out of her hand onto the floor. One of the deputies reached out to take her arm, but she stepped back. "Don't touch me!"

"Ma'am, you will have to come with us to the station. It's obvious that you've wounded your husband with that knife." He produced handcuffs from his pants pocket.

"He deserved it. He's running around with some floozie. I'd do it again and again if I had the chance," she screamed, looking from one man to the next. Acting like a cornered animal, Lola continued her rant as one of the officers forcefully held her while the another applied the cuffs.

"You got a robe or coat to wear?" the larger of the four men asked Lola.

Lola slung her head in the direction of the bathroom. The officer went there and retrieved a blue chenille bathrobe from behind the door, which he placed over her shoulders.

"Call the EMTs for him," one of the officers said to another, pointing at Marc, sitting nearby in an ugly beige chair, acting meek.

Someone had given him a towel to catch the blood and placed him in a chair to wait.

Penelope stepped back from the door as two men hurriedly ushered Lola from the unit. But she wasn't done with the theatrics. Lola began screaming at the top of her lungs as they waited for the elevator to come up to the eighth floor.

"You don't understand," she cried. "I love him. He's my man, not hers. She can't have him."

When the doors opened, two officers walked out, followed by LuAnn. The sight of her nemesis ignited Lola into an even higher decibel of ugly rants.

"I'll kill you, too!" Lola screamed. "You wait till I get out and see if I don't come after you!"

LuAnn looked shocked by the scene before her. She tried to edge toward her unit without coming close to Lola or the police while the officers were holding onto the crazed woman as she vigorously struggled to get free to attack LuAnn. The bathrobe on her shoulders tumbled to the floor during the scuffle.

"Move on, ma'am, please," said one of the men to LuAnn.

As soon as the singer was clear of the elevator cubical, the officers pushed Lola inside the elevator ahead of them. One reached for the robe and carried it along as the doors closed. The next time the elevator opened, Penelope saw the medics arrive carrying medical cases. Not knowing if she would be able to sleep after all the commotion, she decided to watch while the two medics, a man and a woman, bandaged Marc sufficiently to transport him to the emergency room. Two more people exited the elevator later with a stretcher for Marc.

Once Marc was loaded onto the elevator, Penelope walked back into her unit, her slippered feet shuffling along. What a night! Now that everything was quiet, she would try to sleep.

THIRTY-FOUR

BY THE TIME Rachel made it into the office the next morning, the entire condo was abuzz. She hadn't seen everyone acting this crazy since the murder. Then they had reason to be concerned, but now they were shocked by the events caused by one neighbor.

Six messages were on the answering machine. She knew that in mere seconds the residents would be clamoring into her office. *Brace yourself, girl!*

Penelope wasn't one of the neighbors initially present because she had called Rachel very early in the morning to tell her what had occurred while she was sleeping. Rachel had all the information from an eye witness, whom she knew to be reliable. Penelope never lied, never exaggerated. However, Rachel was anxious to hear details from the detective. Would the Rogers be released to return to their units? Would Lola be kept in jail? What about Marc? Had he been seriously injured?

Ruby and Loretta popped in, followed by Olivia and Tia. Everyone was talking at once, so Rachel was getting frustrated. Various other residents came in expressing concern and curiosity. It was a highly disruptive morning. And then Joe appeared. She didn't have to explain anything to him because she had already shared Penelope's conversation earlier.

"Joe!" she stood up from the desk. "This place is crazy. Go with me to the Rogers' unit."

"Of course."

The two ushered everyone from the office and locked the door quickly before anyone else arrived wanting to know what was happening. They opened the door to 809 carefully.

"Should we be in here?" Joe asked.

"No one has told me not to come in. I don't know that a crime was committed. I do manage these units, so I think I need to see the disaster they created. But don't touch anything, Joe. We don't need a repeat of the last time we traipsed through a crime scene," Rachel said, remembering that situation with embarrassment.

"Wasn't planning to."

They stepped over and around broken glass and dishes as best they could. Rachel pulled out her cell phone and proceeded to take pictures of the indescribable mess.

"The Morgans will have an absolute cow when they see these pictures," she said.

"I think it's time to remove Marc and Lola," Joe suggested.

"Absolutely! Detective France shouldn't have a problem with eviction now. I plan to tell the Morgans this has been ongoing and they must evict them if they ever want to have a condo to live in. These nutty people are destroying this unit," Rachel said, stepping around a trash can.

Joe silently nodded his agreement.

"See the blood?" she asked, pointing at the floor. "Lola stabbed Marc in the stomach, also gave him a gash in his thigh. Then she told the police he deserved it. What an idiot."

The majority of damage appeared to be in the living room and dining room. The rest of the rooms seemed to be okay.

"Let's go back down and I'll call the Morgans. They need to get moving on the eviction," Rachel said. "Immediately."

. . .

Rachel sat in her desk chair to listen to the messages that had since come in while they were upstairs. One was from Detective France. She called him back immediately.

"Rachel Barnes, returning your call, Detective. So, what's the news?"

"Okay," France began. "Marc is in the hospital. He'll live. Lola didn't do serious damage to his internal organs, but she definitely inflicted some injury. He's had a little surgery and was stitched up any place she cut him. Lola fared better. Only minor cuts and bruises. However, she's in jail awaiting arraignment."

"What are the charges against them?" Rachel asked.

"Marc, domestic abuse. After they release him from the hospital and take him to jail, he can bond out. Lola, attempted murder. She's not going anywhere."

"Funny, I thought Marc was the bad guy in the picture. Turns out it's Lola. Murder, really?" Rachel was a little surprised.

"I'm afraid so, second degree. And she threatened to kill one of the neighbors, so that will be added onto the list," he said, clearing his throat.

"Unbelievable. And all for jealousy. How foolish," Rachel said.

"I'm going to ask Marc a few questions about Lola's jealousy," the detective said. "It appears out of control."

"I'm sure the neighbor can give you a good description of what Lola's jealousy looks like, too. Lola *is* over the top. Even came to my office to complain about Marc's philandering," she said. "Oh, and I am asking the owners of the unit to evict them. Are you okay with that? You weren't the last time I wanted to."

"Eviction takes time, so go ahead with your plans," he answered, "However, Marc is the only one going to be affected by the eviction. Lola's probably going to be in jail pending trial."

"Okay, I will follow through. Thanks for keeping me in the loop," she said.

After she hung up the phone, Rachel's next call was to the Morgans.

About ten days later, around two o'clock, Marc walked into Rachel's office.

"Hi, Rachel."

"Hey, Marc. I see you're out of jail."

"Yeah, about that. I need to talk to you."

"Good, because I need to talk to you, too."

Marc sat in the chair and sighed. He was cleaned up, wearing decent clothes, but he looked uncomfortable.

"I got out last night. I didn't try to bond out, I just admitted what I'd done and let the judge sentence me." Marc appeared to relax as he started talking.

"So, what was your sentence?"

"Actually, it was pretty much time served, a fine, and probation. The Public Defender blamed my beating up on Lola as self-defense. I don't think the judge totally bought that reasoning, but there was some truth there, considering she tried to kill me."

"I see," Rachel said. She could understand the rationale there. A knife wielding woman coming after a person would provoke you to defend yourself. And maybe add in a few extra punches during the heat of anger.

"Now I'm on probation."

"How are your injuries?"

"I'm healing okay," Marc said, gently patting his midsection. "They weren't deep cuts, so I was lucky."

"You do realize you'll have to move out of the unit?" Rachel had to tell him at some point.

"I kinda thought you might say that."

"The Morgans have started the eviction process. They couldn't get in touch with you, so they had no choice." Rachel was flipping a pencil back and forth between two fingers as she talked.

"I understand. It's okay. I plan to move."

"Let the Morgans know that, please."

"I will."

"Good. What about Lola?" Rachel was quite curious over the situation the woman had placed herself in.

Marc ran his hand through his hair and sighed. "She's in jail and I don't expect her to get out any time soon. Maybe never."

"Really?"

"Yeah, and there are other charges pending."

"What do you mean?"

"Well, the detective talked to me in jail. They're doing diagnostic tests -- if that's the right word -- on the knife she stuck me with. And he said something about a meat tenderizer. I don't understand it all. But he asked me a lot of questions."

Rachel understood about the meat tenderizer, but she didn't share what she knew with Marc.

"So, does she have an attorney?"

"We don't have that kinda money. But her Public Defender seems like he knows what he's doing." Marc looked back at her as if to suggest everything was organized.

"I understand, but she's facing an attempted murder charge, plus more, you just said. Don't you think she should have a decent attorney?" She stopped flipping the pencil, staring at him.

"We don't have the money!" he said, raising his voice along with an exaggerated shrug of his shoulders. "Where am I going to get that kinda money? We don't even own a house."

Rachel looked him squarely in the eyes. "Do you want her to get off, Marc?"

Marc looked down quickly. It was apparent to Rachel that he didn't care if his wife was ever released from jail.

"Okay, there we go. You don't want her to get out. You're afraid she'll stab you in your sleep, aren't you?" Rachel knew this was his thought. He was only interested in protecting himself.

Marc shifted awkwardly in the chair. Rachel shook her head in disgust. *Why do people torture each other? Why not get a divorce? They certainly didn't stay together because of religious reasons.*

"So, when will you be out of the unit?"

"This week."

"And you're going to clean up that mess you made in the unit before you leave, right?"

Marc nodded enthusiastically. "Yeah, oh, sure. I already planned to do that."

But he answered too quickly to be believed. Rachel leaned across the desk.

"You leave that unit like it's brand spanking new," she said, with all the intimidation she could muster in her tone. "I don't care if you have to hire an entire cleaning crew to get the job done."

"Yes, ma'am." Marc answered her strict tone with a very agreeable one. He attempted to smile, but failed.

“Now leave.”

“Right.” Marc stood, looking down at her. “Nice knowing you.”

“I wish I could say the same.”

He closed the door softly behind as he walked out.

THIRTY-FIVE

ALL FOUR GIRLS were gathered for lunch at one of the cute restaurants that the tourists flocked to during the winter season. It wasn't exactly the winter season, so acquiring a table was easy since they were early.

"Oh, that one over there by the window," said Olivia, pointing in the direction of her idea of the perfect table.

Everyone rushed to the indicated table, claiming seats quickly before the locals came in for lunch.

"Perfect," Olivia said, smiling her satisfaction and reaching for the menu on the table.

"Good job," Rachel said, scooting her chair.

"Y'all, I'm famished!" LuAnn said. "I haven't had breakfast."

"I had breakfast, but that was hours ago," Tia said. "I'm starved."

Each perused their menus. The server came to the table, her pad in hand and pen poised for their orders.

"I want to order a glass of iced tea," Olivia said, looking up at the server. "And the Caesar salad with chicken."

"Separate checks," Tia said. "I'll have the same as her, Caesar salad with chicken, but no croutons, please."

LuAnn looked up at the woman. "Make mine an iced tea, please. I want the chicken strips salad."

"Me, too," Rachel said. "And water."

All three women looked at Rachel.

"Aren't you having your famous iced tea?" Olivia asked.

"Nope. Nothing with sugar in it." Rachel looked back at the ladies with a very pleased expression on her face. But she knew she couldn't get away with that simple answer.

"Okay, here's the deal," she started, leaning back in her chair after the server left the table. "I found out recently, after a trip to the hospital, that I am a diabetic. I can't drink anything with sugar in it. Well, not if I want to regulate myself."

Silence fell on the table, like a black cloud blocking out the sun. No one dared say a word. Had they heard her correctly? Diabetes?

"I was having issues. Remember, I ate chocolate bars and cookies and pastry when we were at the clubhouse? And my iced tea had lots of sugar packets in it. I was feeling faint, dizzy, and I was thirsty all the time. Not to mention, my exhaustion was through the roof. I had the symptoms, and my habits were exacerbating my condition, but I didn't want to go to the doctor."

"I remember you saying that," Tia said. "Why didn't you say something to me?"

"I guess I didn't want to hear bad news," she said. "But I landed in the hospital, and that's when they discovered my condition. I probably would have eventually gone to the doctor, because I was researching my symptoms and I suspected I had diabetes. But I was stubborn. You know how I can be."

LuAnn was the first to speak. "I think it's commendable of you, honey, to own up to your mistake."

Olivia silently stared at Rachel. She seemed in a state of disbelief.

"Actually, it all worked out for the best, except for the part where I've been diagnosed with diabetes. Joe thought I was getting drunk when I wasn't. That caused a problem between us, which I mentioned to you before. Remember, I told you I was sleeping in the spare bedroom?"

The server returned with their beverages and left. Everyone remained silent until Rachel resumed her story.

"We ended up rarely speaking to each other and, let's just say, life was chilly. But I kept going out with you girls and being stubborn and defiant." Rachel looked at her glass of water. "I was rebelling. I was determined that Joe was not going to tell me what to do."

"So, the diagnosis turned you around," suggested Tia.

"Yes. And my talk with Loretta. I started to see my error and how I wasn't treating my husband well. And then we went to church."

"Really?" said Olivia, suddenly perking up.

"Yes. It was even my suggestion. Loretta had encouraged me to attend. And I liked it. I really liked it, and I slowly began to accept the fact that I had a problem. So, that's when I did some research and found out my symptoms were probably diabetes. But before I could go to the doctor, I had an incident in the bathtub. I could have drowned due to my stupidity, but Joe rescued me."

"We wondered why you hadn't joined us for drinks several times now," said Tia. "But I am so glad you found help before it became even more dangerous for your health."

"Me too," Olivia said. "I'm so proud of you. And you're going to church," She was obviously pleased about that change.

"Honey, you're the best!" LuAnn said, patting Rachel's arm.

"Thanks," Rachel said, bowing her head a little from embarrassment. "I need support, so thank you."

"We're here for you, honey," LuAnn said. "What are friends for?"

When the salads arrived, each dove in with gusto, and appreciation of their friend. Rachel knew that they would support her in their own way. After all, that's what friends are for.

Detective France walked into Rachel's office, unannounced. Rachel only had time to plug in the coffee pot before he came in.

"Oh, my, you are most definitely an early bird," she said.

The detective grinned at her. "I've been known to be so."

"Would you like a cup of coffee?"

"Sure."

"Give it a few minutes, I just plugged the pot in," she said. "How is your wife and the baby?"

"Well," he said, a giant smile crossing his face. "She's just a few months away. We're both really excited, this being our first."

"I am sure of that." Rachel liked the detective a lot. She was very pleased about the expansion of their family.

"Some friends are throwing showers and all of that baby stuff. It's an exciting time for us."

"Aw, that's so sweet!"

"But, enough of that. I'm here today to give you a small update."

"I see."

"But first, about your resident, Marc."

"What about him?"

"Has he moved all of his belongings out?"

"Supposedly, he has. The Morgans have stopped eviction because he's willing to leave." Rachel reached behind her for two mugs. "And he's supposed to have been out since yesterday. I haven't had a chance to check the unit this morning."

Rachel poured out two cups of coffee for herself and the detective. She handed one of the mugs to him.

"Thank you. Can't ever get enough coffee."

"I'm not sure if he cleaned up inside or not," she said, taking a sip of the coffee. "I told him to."

"Do you want to go check the unit now?" he asked, taking a sip of coffee.

"With you? Sure, sounds like a good idea."

They rose from their chairs, coffee mugs in hand, and moved toward the door. The detective held it open for Rachel and they walked to the elevator. Rachel really hoped for a beautiful baby to be born to him and his wife. He deserved that much in his line of work.

When they arrived on the eighth floor, Penelope was walking down the walkway toward them.

"Hi, Penelope," Rachel said.

Penelope nodded in response to the two of them.

"Are you okay?" Rachel asked.

"I'm fine. I'm enjoying the peace and quiet for a change," she said with a smile.

"So, I gather Marc did leave yesterday as scheduled?" she asked.

"He sure did. And I was delighted," she said. "If I'd had pompoms, I'd have been waving them in the air as he left."

The two grinned over her humor.

"Do you know if he cleaned up inside?"

"A lot of trash went out, I saw that," Penelope said, placing her hand under her chin in a contemplative move. "As to cleaning up the rest, beats me."

"We're going to look inside now," Rachel told her.

"Okay. Please make the next tenant quieter," Penelope said.

"I will certainly try to do that, Penelope." The old lady definitely deserved a new, quiet neighbor after her many restless nights.

The detective and Rachel entered the unit and stood at the entrance, looking at the environment. While the breakage and trash had been removed, the furniture, which belonged to the Morgans, was not in good shape. It had not been reorganized in an ordinary manner around the room, nor had it been cleaned or dusted. Scars in the wood were visible due to the objects being thrown around. Rachel sighed.

"The Morgans will not be happy with this damage. And the walls!" She pointed at obvious injury to one of the walls.

Rachel ran her hands down parts of the wall that had gouges. Other areas still had blood stained patches. She didn't touch them. Obviously, Marc hadn't bothered to wash the walls before he left.

Rachel turned to the detective. "This is such a mess."

"Yeah, I see that. At least he took out the trash."

"Humph. Barely. All he did was pick up the breakage of *their* possessions. What about what belonged to the Morgans?" Rachel's hands waved in the air with frustration. "They ruined some of the furniture. For all I know, the couch has glass slivers in it."

"Yeah, not good."

"The Morgans are going to be very unhappy about this," Rachel said. "They'll have to come back to re-rent this place now. They can't rent it like this, not without more cleanup and painting being done. Maybe replace some furniture."

"I think you're right," France said.

They headed to the front door and walked toward the elevator, talking.

"We're testing the knife Lola used to stab Marc," the detective said.

"Yes, Marc mentioned that to me. What is the purpose of that?"

"It's just something we do."

"Really? I bet there's more to it than that." Rachel grinned after her statement, but the detective didn't crack a smile. "Oh, come on! And what happened with the diary I gave you?"

"Well, the contents confirm that Marc was spending time with Eneida. There could be a connection to her murder," he answered. "I really can't say much more."

"No one knew she was seeing him."

"She wasn't exactly seeing him; it was more stalking than anything else," he finally revealed.

"Stalking? Then why didn't she tell someone? Tell me? Tell the police?" Rachel couldn't understand why her friend had not confided in her.

"Hard to say."

"So, Marc did kill Eneida, as some of us suspected?"

"I didn't say that. He's our lead suspect, though."

Rachel stopped in front of the elevator before pushing the button.

"You're being evasive."

"Let's just say, wait until the test results come back on the knife – and the meat tenderizer." Detective France pushed the button.

Rachel looked up at the detective, frowning at him.

"Patience, Rachel. More than one person had access to that knife. And we don't know about the meat tenderizer. Have a little patience."

"But you said Marc was stalking her. Why aren't you anxious to find him?"

"I didn't say we didn't know where he is."

"Oh."

Rachel sighed in exasperation. It was obvious that the detective wasn't going to be forthcoming. She would have to be patient, which was not her strong suit. They traveled down in the elevator in silence.

THIRTY-SIX

RACHEL SAT on the balcony of her unit, a cup of coffee at her side on the table. In her lap she had a Bible. Actually, it was Joe's Bible. Rachel had never touched it before. Joe was the one who saw value in reading scripture. It wasn't until recently that Rachel had felt the need to turn the first page in this big book. And it was a big book, filled with letters bouncing back at her in black and red. She felt beckoned to opened it.

...He asked him, "Do you want to get well?"

She had randomly opened the book to wherever it happened to fall. And fall it did, to John 5:6. Here Jesus was asking an invalid man who was lying beside the Pool of Bethesda if he wanted to be healed. Of course, he did, the man just couldn't get into the pool at the appropriate time without assistance. So, Jesus healed him. The man picked up his mat and walked away.

Rachel raised her head to look out into the beautiful blue sky before her.

"Do you want to get well?"

Her thoughts ran through that short sentence, combing each word like she carefully did when grooming each hair on Rufus' body.

The hairs on your head...

Rachel recalled something about the number of hairs on the head, sparrows falling, but God knew everything. She didn't know where that thought had come from. Childhood? Perhaps. Certainly not in recent years had she given any thought to what was contained in this big book. But she had somehow remembered that God knew her. God knew the number of hairs on her head. Even on *her* head, a head that couldn't have cared less about God, church or the Bible. Even her.

Rachel looked back down at the Bible in her lap, lying welcomingly open. Joe had said to start with the book of John. She paged back to the beginning of John. And she began to read.

An hour later, Rachel decided it was time she reintroduced herself to God. She knew He had not forgotten her in all the years following childhood, but for herself, she felt like she needed to initiate contact. To be healed, in her soul and body. Loretta had encouraged her to go to church, and she had. Joe always wanted her to go with him, but she didn't see the need. Well, now she saw the need. She needed to rely on Him as her support, her guide, her counselor.

"Remember me? The munchkin in Sunday school? Yeah, I haven't been around for a long time, have I? I'm sorry. Really, I am. Life just got in my way. Well, I let life get in my way, didn't I? There were more important things to do, to see, to be, I guess. At least that's what I thought at the time." Rachel sighed and began again. "I know I'm supposed to put You first. I get it. But I haven't done that. Far from it. But I'm told it's never too late. I can begin again. So, here I am, Lord. Beginning again. I'm at Your feet asking You to help me be a good woman, a good wife, a good condo manager, a good friend. Just plain good.

"Joe deserves a devoted wife. An understanding wife. Yeah, I know, I have to do this for me. I get that. But he does deserve a better behaving wife. Please help me to turn away from the distractions that tempt me in other directions. My poor body will thank You, too. Joe will thank You for the strength I find in You. He is so pleased with my devotion to the church and learning about the Bible. He's thrilled, and I am so happy he is happy with the changes in me. And I'm really liking church. Can't believe I just said that, but it's true."

Rachel smiled as she again cast her eyes onto the view of puffy clouds floating along so leisurely in the beautiful blue sky. All created by God. A universe she could not completely see, but knew existed. She was created by God. She was a child of God. Awesome. Simply awesome.

Ron and Arlene Morgan were dragging out a beat-up and stained beige chair from the unit once rented by Lola and Marc Rogers. They had come into town from their other residence in New York State to handle the destruction to their unit. They planned to dump most of the furniture, since it was damaged beyond repair. It wasn't even decent enough to donate to Goodwill. The appliances were acceptable, but the walls needed repair and paint. The curtains were ripped and destroyed, and the floors also required repair. It was a discouraging scene.

LuAnn walked by as they were manhandling the chair out the door.

"Oh, my, y'all must be the Morgans," LuAnn said with a big smile.

"Yes, I'm Ron, this is my wife Arlene," the man said, reaching out a hand toward her.

LuAnn took his hand and reached over to Arlene to shake her hand as well.

"Nice to meet you folks," she said. "I live on the other side of the elevators."

"Oh, so you own one of the units?" Arlene asked.

"No, I just rent. I'd like to own one, they're so nice -- and quiet now that these people left."

"I'm sorry our tenants caused you grief," Ron said, genuinely concerned.

"Oh, it wasn't your fault, honey. They were just, well, a bit trashy."

"Would you like to buy our unit?" The look on Arlene's face said that she had just had the thought.

"Me? Hmm. I don't know. I hadn't thought about this unit," LuAnn said, cocking her head to the side.

"Well, we have to rent it or sell it. I think we'd prefer to sell it so we don't have this problem again," he said, looking at his wife for agreement.

"Yes, selling would be preferable," Arlene agreed.

"We'd make you a good deal, under market value. You see, with our grandkids in New York, this really isn't convenient for us anymore," Ron said, motioning toward the unit.

"Well..." LuAnn said.

"Since we have to paint all the walls anyway, you could choose the colors you would prefer," Arlene said. "Really make it your place."

LuAnn was not known for deep thinking or procrastination. She was a spontaneous woman with a creative nature. Choosing the colors for her apartment was a very appealing idea. The unit she lived in now was barely acceptable with its colors. Actually, there was no color. Every wall was brown. LuAnn didn't consider brown a color. It was dull and dark. But it was a rental, after all. Here she would own the unit, not just rent. She was very tempted.

The Morgans could see she was mulling over their proposal.

"How much would you want down?" LuAnn asked.

"$10,000?" Ron said.

"I can do that," LuAnn said.

Arlene mentioned a price she knew to be below the true value of the unit. She even offered to hold the mortgage. A couple heartbeats went by before LuAnn spoke.

"You've got a deal!" LuAnn said, reaching her hand out again to shake on it.

Ron and Arlene broke out in smiles and actually cheered.

"We'll have our attorney draw up the paperwork," Ron said.

"Terrific! And I'll go to the paint store and pick up paint chips. I can't believe it. I just bought a condo!"

THIRTY-SEVEN

THE GIRLS WERE CELEBRATING the acquisition of LuAnn's condo unit at their favorite place, the clubhouse. Everyone was toasting and cheering. Rachel drank an unsweetened iced tea.

"I don't even have to move to another floor," LuAnn said. "I can just trot my belongings down the walkway; so easy."

"Are they leaving any furniture for you? Do you need any furniture?" Olivia asked.

"Most of the furniture is old or was torn up by the Rogers, so it's going in the dumpster." LuAnn answered. "I don't really need any furniture, but the second bedroom set they have I am taking for my extra bedroom. They must not have used that room much at all."

"Good idea," Tia said.

"I'm delighted you're becoming a permanent resident," Olivia said.

"Me, too," Rachel said.

"Now I just need a fella," LuAnn threw out there, tapping her red nails on the side of her mug.

The girls giggled.

"Speaking of fellas," Rachel said, turning her gaze on Olivia. "You haven't caught us up on your romance with the good doctor lately. What's up?"

Olivia quickly looked down at her lap, poked her head back up and smiled politely. The kind of smile one uses when trying to come across sincere, yet not revealing too much.

"My doctor friend is so busy with his grown children and his grandchildren..."

"He has grandchildren?" interrupted Rachel.

"I told you that."

"No, you didn't," Tia said.

"Well, whatever, now you know he has grandchildren," Olivia said, fussing with her necklace. "So, his family keeps him busy. And mine keeps me busy."

"Since when?" Rachel asked.

Olivia huffed out a breath of frustration and glared over at Rachel.

"Robert moved back to Florida and he's only an hour away." Robert was Olivia's oldest son.

"When did that happen?" Tia asked.

"I don't know, not long," Olivia said, getting more annoyed as the truth was finally coming out. "So, he's been coming around. And Nancy is making noises of moving closer with her family, too. So, I'll get to see *my* grandchildren far more often now."

"What you're saying, honey, is that family comes first," LuAnn said.

"Yes!" Olivia looked at LuAnn with appreciation. She understood.

"And so how does all of this family bonding affect your relationship?" Rachel asked. "If he's with his kids and grandkids, you're spending time with Robert, and here comes Nancy back into the picture soon with your grandchildren, what happens to you and the doctor?"

"Well, we had a little talk and agreed to cancel the cruise. We don't have time for a trip right now. And since then, I haven't been seeing very much of him," Olivia said, putting her glass back on the table. She looked at each of her girlfriends faces carefully. "Truthfully, I haven't seen him in three weeks. And, funny thing, I don't mind. It's all good."

No one spoke among the table of friends. They were a little surprised that Olivia was coping so well.

"You know, honey," LuAnn said, breaking the silence and winking at Olivia, "I think that means you'll have more time for us. So, you can help me move!"

All the girls laughed and hoisted their drinks.

"Cheers to that!"

"So, what is happening in the murder investigation?" Tia asked Rachel. "You haven't said anything much lately."

"What I'm being told is that the knife Lola used to cut Marc with is being tested. That's normal. Also, the meat tenderizer someone used to assault LuAnn. And, you won't believe this," Rachel said, "but the diary I found in Eneida's unit has some interesting content. It implicates Marc."

"How so?" Olivia asked.

"He was stalking Eneida." Rachel looked from one shocked face to the other.

"Stalking!" LuAnn said.

"I'm afraid so."

"Did Eneida tell you Marc was stalking her? She didn't tell me," Tia said.

"No, I didn't know a thing," Rachel said. "The first I heard of it was from the detective."

"She was always so private," Tia said.

"Didn't you read any of her diary before you gave it to Detective France?" Olivia asked.

"No, of course not. I didn't want my fingerprints on it." Rachel said, swirling her ice cubes around with a straw.

"Well, I'm not shocked he was stalking her," LuAnn said. "He was kinda stalking me, too."

"Yes, he was," Rachel agreed.

"So, Marc did it!" Tia said.

"Detective France wouldn't confirm that. Not until they get test results from the knife and meat tenderizer."

"He did it; I said that all along. Marc killed Eneida." Tia raised her glass into the air for emphasis. "It's just a matter of time until he's arrested."

"Don't go saying that to anyone. Keep that opinion between us, okay?" Rachel said.

"Of course. But that's the murderer," Tia insisted.

"I've always been suspicious of that strange man lurking around with a hat on and wearing a long coat," Olivia said. "No one wears a long coat in Florida, even during the cooler months. And a hat!"

"Did y'all ever hear who that man was? Why he was hanging around here?" LuAnn asked.

"I've never been told anything about him," Rachel said.

"I think he's connected to our Miss Loretta," Olivia said. "Who knows who might come looking for a former detective? He's probably a hit man. I'll bet he's with the Mafia, or some other crime syndicate."

Rachel looked over at Olivia. "Really? You have to jump to the conclusion that man was with the Mafia? I highly doubt it."

"If it wasn't Marc, it was that strange man," Tia said. "He could have been released from prison and came looking for Loretta. Very possible."

"There's always Jorge," LuAnn suggested. "He could be the one."

"I will not discuss Jorge as a potential suspect," Rachel said. "It is *not* him. He's too kind."

"And quiet. As they say, you have to watch out for the quiet ones," Olivia said.

"I don't care what you say, I cannot believe that nice man is a killer," Rachel insisted. "We'll just have to have patience, as the detective told me, until we are informed about who killed Eneida."

"It was Marc," Tia persisted.

"Okay, enough. So, everyone is helping me move to my new place?" LuAnn interjected.

Each made a resounding affirmative agreement.

"I better not break a nail," LuAnn said.

One week later, the girls joined forces and moved LuAnn from her rental unit to her new, freshly painted condo just down the walkway. LuAnn had found a permanent home all her own, and great friends as a bonus. She couldn't have been happier.

THIRTY-EIGHT

DETECTIVE FRANCE ENTERED Rachel's office, right at his scheduled time.

"Morning, Rachel," He said, nodding. "I have some good news."

"So you said on the phone. You're going to tell me who killed Eneida?"

"Yes, and that I've filed charges for murder one," he said, sitting in the chair.

Rachel was impatient to know. "Well, tell me, who did it?"

The detective answered with one word, "Lola."

Rachel fell back into her chair, silenced from shock and slack jawed.

"She was right under our noses all along. And I'll take a bottle of water, if you don't mind," he said.

Rachel reached behind her chair for the mini fridge, opening the door.

"How is that possible? She's such a meek, beaten-down woman who was abused by her low- life husband," Rachel said, handing the bottle to the detective, also taking one for herself.

"Apparently, she wasn't as meek as everyone thought she was,"

Detective France said, unscrewing the cap on the bottle. "She had jealousy pumping fuel into her."

"Jealousy? Okay, I understand that part, but how could she have been jealous of Eneida?" Rachel looked confused.

"When I talked to Marc, he said that Lola was a highly jealous woman. Marc could barely look sideways at a woman, any female, it seems," he said, taking a drink from the bottle. "She would seethe over nothing, waiting until they returned home so she could scream at him."

"And throw things."

"That too. Marc did say she threw things at him in a jealous rage. It was her alone who threw the stuff, not him," the detective said. "He said she even sneaked up on him while he slept to inflict injuries. Some of his bruises and cuts were from her night terror attacks on him."

"And sometimes he hit her back in defense?"

"Probably, most of the time. Except when she attacked while he slept," France said.

"I don't understand the jealousy toward Eneida in particular, a jealousy that is big enough to kill over. She was not friendly with that couple, and she didn't like Marc," Rachel said.

"By talking to Marc, I found out there was more going on than anyone else knew," he answered. "Marc admitted visiting Eneida, uninvited, on numerous occasions. That was also documented in the diary. He said that she was always polite to him, but hustled him back out the door after their conversations. Eneida made it clear to him that she was not interested in his attention."

"She never mentioned his visits to any of her friends, me included," Rachel said.

"Eneida possibly didn't take it too seriously, yet she knew he was stalking her," the detective said. "She made it clear in the diary that she felt him looking at her when she walked down the walkway, and it made her uncomfortable. Marc didn't want that information getting back to Lola. He'd be in for a pounding for sure. Eneida also wrote that during his intermittent visits, he was always pleasant enough, so she never mentioned them to anyone. She did not feel he would harm her."

"She was right about that. So, Marc was the visitor her daughter mentioned?"

"It appears so."

"But Lola must have known he was making clandestine visits," she said.

"Marc said she somehow suspected because he would receive more cuts and bruises after each visit." France crossed his legs before edging back in the chair.

"What a dummy! You would think he'd take no for an answer and behave himself," she said.

"According to Marc, he has always had a restless spirit. I would say his so-called restless spirit was more of a consistently wandering eye. Lola had reason to be jealous," France said.

"How did you find out Lola killed Eneida?" she asked, taking sips of water.

"Combining Marc's statements and the diary content with the test results on the knife, it became clear. The knife she used to stab Marc in their latest fracas was the same one used to kill Eneida. We have DNA proof. We were also able to tie the meat tenderizer to Eneida's murder."

"I don't believe it!"

"We never found the object used to beat Eneida before she was killed. But after forensics tested the meat tenderizer used to attack LuAnn, evidence was found to connect that item to Eneida's murder," he said, taking several swallows of water. "The fingerprints were smeared on it – except for the thumbprint," he said.

"Lola's?"

"Yes, the print was a perfect match to Lola," the detective said. "Also, fine wooden splinters found on Eneida's body and head perfectly matched the meat tenderizer. So, that was an important find and a blunder on Lola's part."

"Okay, so here's my question: Did Marc know Lola killed Eneida?" Rachel asked, leaning forward in her chair.

"I don't have any evidence pointing to that. Marc claimed he was suspicious after we found Eneida's body, but he never asked Lola outright if she did it. Basically, he didn't want to know," the detective said. "If he knew and didn't say anything, he'd be an accomplice after the fact and both of them would go to jail. So, he never asked the big question."

"Well, I'm relieved," Rachel said. "What does this mean for Lola?"

"She'll go to trial for murder one on Eneida, attempted murder of her husband, and making threats to kill LuAnn, plus attacking her with that meat tenderizer."

"Wow."

"I'm sure she'll do some long prison time, assuming the jury finds her guilty," he said. "And I'm certain the jury will come to the right conclusion."

"Another dummy. Who commits murder and decides to keep the knife she committed murder with in the kitchen drawer? Why? To carve meat? Not such a brilliant thought process! Dogs are smarter than that."

The detective smiled slightly at the last remark. "My dog certainly is."

"Even goofy Rufus is brighter than that. I am well pleased, Detective France," Rachel said with a smile of satisfaction. "Terrific work piecing it all together."

"The murder case is closed now, so you can relax," he said. "The culprit wasn't a Mafia hitman, an old lover or any other imaginary event. It was a jealous woman."

"Wait till I tell Joe!"

THIRTY-NINE

THE NEXT MORNING, Rachel emailed a letter to all the residents informing them of the conclusion of the murder case. She knew this would cause everyone to go buzzing about the situation all over again. But at least they wouldn't be conjuring up schemes of maniacal murderers trying to break into the condo building. Everyone could go back to their normal lives, whatever that looked like.

As Rachel was turning to another task, a couple of women strolled into her office, arm in arm.

"Good day, Rachel," Loretta said. As usual, she looked elegant, dressed in a black pantsuit with white piping around the collar. Rachel probably wouldn't recognize her dressed any other way.

Standing beside Loretta was Ruby, still holding the arm in arm pose.

Will wonders never cease?

"Ladies! So nice to see you both," she said. "And so friendly, I might add."

Both of the women laughed softly.

"We figured it was time to bury the hatchet and be friends," Ruby said with a big smile on her face. "We've only known each other for sixty years, for crying in the beer. What were we waiting for?" Ruby said, hiding her brazenness under a white swimsuit coverup, which she seemed to have adopted lately when in public.

Loretta was all smiles, too.

"Our pasts are in the past," Loretta said. "We don't have decades left, so why not become sisters at long last?"

Rachel sat still, smiling, as she listened intently to the women. This news made her heart happy.

"We're both alone with no family, so we decided to become family to each other," Ruby said, patting Loretta's hand that was resting at her elbow.

"Well, ladies, I am surprised, but pleasantly so," Rachel said. "I thought you two were mortal enemies or something close to that. I am very proud of both of you."

They thanked Rachel in unison.

"So, is this why you two came in today, to tell me you kissed and made up?" Rachel asked.

"Yes, and to tell you that we're going on a trip together, so you need to know our units will be vacant for a period of time," Loretta said.

"We don't want any crazy murderers hanging out in our units while we're gone," Ruby said.

"You don't have to worry about that anymore," Rachel advised them. "There never was a crazy murderer roaming around. The person who killed Eneida was none other than Lola. I just found out late yesterday."

The women dropped their arms to their sides in surprise, staring back at Rachel with astonished faces.

"Lola!" they said in unison.

"Yes, ladies, it was Lola."

Loretta and Ruby looked at each other and then back at Rachel.

"How? Why?" Ruby asked

"Basically, Lola was a very jealous woman, and Marc had a wandering eye," Rachel answered. "He visited Eneida, but she spurned his attention. Unfortunately, Lola knew Marc had visited Eneida, so she killed off what she saw as competition. End of story."

"Lola. You're sure you're not incorrectly using her name and you really mean someone else?" Loretta asked.

"I know what you're thinking." Rachel smiled. "But it really was Lola. Apparently, she had a wicked, jealous temper. And her jealousy fueled a murderous rage. So, she whacked Eneida around with a meat tenderizer and then knifed her."

Loretta and Ruby stood silently again, staring at Rachel.

"I'll be," Loretta finally said.

"Me too be," Ruby said. "But why use a meat tenderizer? Wasn't the knife enough?"

"Lola probably wanted to subdue her so she could kill her easily. After being beat up, I doubt Eneida had any strength left to fight Lola."

"That makes sense," Ruby said.

"Now you ladies can go on your trip and not have to worry about a random maniac busting into your unit while you're out of town. Okay? Feel better now?"

Loretta started to smile. "Actually, yes, I really do."

"Me, too," Ruby said.

"So, where are you ladies traveling to?" Rachel asked.

Ruby eagerly spoke first. "Well, we have quite the trip planned out! First, we fly to California. We're going to see some sights in Hollywood."

"Grauman's Chinese Theatre, where all the movie stars have their handprints," interrupted Loretta.

"Then we take a cruise over to Hawaii where we will stay for a week in Honolulu at a luxury hotel," Ruby continued.

"We plan to eat ourselves silly on the cruise," Loretta chimed in. "We have tickets for some entertainment once we're in Honolulu, and we will be touring anything that has importance while there."

"Wow, ladies, that really sounds terrific!" Rachel said. "It sounds like the trip of a lifetime."

"We figure we're not getting any younger, so let's go spend the dough," Ruby said, smiling broadly and shoving one of her bony elbows into Loretta.

"Sounds like a great idea to me, ladies," Rachel said. "And I'll keep everything safe here for your return."

"Thank you so much for all you do, dear," Loretta said. "I trust things are going well in your life?"

"Yes, very much so. All is well between Joe and me and in every other department as well."

"I have noticed you in church regularly on Sundays," said Loretta. "So, I presumed a change had taken place in your life."

"Yes. Our talk helped me a lot," she said. "I later discovered that I have diabetes, but it's under control now."

"That's good to hear, dear." Loretta looked very pleased. "We'll see you when we return. And talk more then."

"Bye, Rachel," Ruby said. "We leave on Wednesday, so you won't see us for a couple weeks."

"I will mark that down on my calendar," Rachel said, reaching for her pencil. "You ladies behave yourselves while on your journey."

"Ha, ha, we sure won't be doing that," Ruby said, laughing and pulling Loretta toward the door.

"See you in a few weeks, dear," Loretta said over her shoulder.

"Bye, ladies."

"I am so pleased with life, Joe. At least at this moment," Rachel said as she reclined in bed, her head propped on a pillow behind her.

"I am, too," Joe said. He was lying beside her in their bed. Even though the TV was on, they weren't paying close attention to it.

"The condo has settled down to its normal heartbeat, the murder is solved, and my personal life is no longer drama ridden," Rachel said, folding her hands across her stomach in satisfaction.

"You've come a long way, baby!" Joe joked. "Getting your blood sugar under control, attending church regularly, reading the Bible, attending Bible studies -- color me impressed."

"There were some tough days, Joe. You know that. It wasn't a slide down the mountain. Rather, it was more like a trudge *up* a mountain getting my blood sugar to behave," she said, adjusting the strap on her favorite blue nightie. "But I got through those hard days where I felt crummy. And those silly chocolate bars! Sheesh, I thought I was going to die unless I ate one. But I didn't. I resisted the urge."

Joe looked at her approvingly. "Good job."

"You were very helpful, Dear."

"I didn't do anything; you did it all."

"With God's help. He gave me the strength to resist temptation, that urge, like Rufus gnawing on his bone. Relentless, ceaseless gnawing, wearing down the foundation. I am trying so hard to eat right."

"And you are persevering."

"Yes. When that overwhelming urge hits me, I say, God help me be strong. And He does."

"Amen."

Rachel rolled on her side so she could fully look at Joe.

"I am the luckiest woman in Florida," she said as she smiled. "I have you, the best, most considerate husband. Most understanding, tolerant man..."

"Wow, that's laying it on a little thick," he interrupted as he rolled over toward the center of the bed to face his wife. "Let's not forget what a strong woman you are. Faithful, kind, loving, a little bit of a sarcastic brat sometimes..."

Rachel's fist burst out, playfully punching him in the gut in one swift move. They started laughing, which brought Rufus to attention. He had been peacefully lying on the floor, but when the playful tussling began, he sprang into action. With one bound of his large form, Rufus landed between the couple, his front paws managing to rest on each body.

"O-w-w-w-w, Rufus!" Rachel cried.

"Ooph! You big brute!" Joe called out.

Of course, Rufus thought they were playing as they tried to get his weight off their bodies. He smacked each with his paws as he continued to be rowdy, bouncing around on the bed, his paws striking wherever they landed. Joe and Rachel were laughing, which only incited the big dog to be more rambunctious.

Meanwhile, Benny was keeping a watchful eye on the commotion from his perch on the dresser. All of a sudden, the bed collapsed loudly onto the floor. The cat howled in dismay and sprang off the dresser. Rufus saw the fleeing cat and darted after him in hot pursuit, tearing half the bedcovers off the bed and dragging them along after him. Rachel and Joe were left looking at each other in disbelief.

"The bed!" Rachel cried out.

"I know!"

"What will the neighbors think?"

"It's not the first time this has happened, and it won't be the last."

Joe looked at his wife sprawled on the uneven bed, with half the sheets missing, the rest flowing onto the floor.

And they laughed.

ABOUT THE AUTHOR

Janie Owens is traditionally and self-published, sometimes under the name Elizabeth. Llewellyn Worldwide released her first of five instructional books in 2000. How To Communicate With Spirits won the Coalition of Visionary Resources 2002 Visionary Award for Biographical/Personal Book. She is now under the wing of Next Chapter Publishing for the release of her first inspirational series.

Some of Janie's interests are reading, painting, and travel. Janie and her husband Vincent believe in adoption of animals. Consequently, they have a houseful of furbabies. Both cats and dogs reside in (mostly) peaceful conditions in their large central Florida home. However, if you've ever owned Chihuahuas, you know that quiet is not often heard. Bina and Peewee keep life interesting for the cats.

Her latest release is 50+ Condo Series: The Murder. Book 2 will be 50+ Condo, The Daughter.

Central Florida is ripe for fantastic book settings and adventure. Join her at the beach by reading one of her books!

Dear reader,

We hope you enjoyed reading *The Murder*. Please take a moment to leave a review, even if it's a short one. Your opinion is important to us.

Discover more books by Janie Owens at https://www.nextchapter.pub/authors/janie-owens

Want to know when one of our books is free or discounted? Join the newsletter at http://eepurl.com/bqqB3H

Best regards,

Janie Owens and the Next Chapter Team

You might also like:
Murder on Tyneside by Eileen Thornton

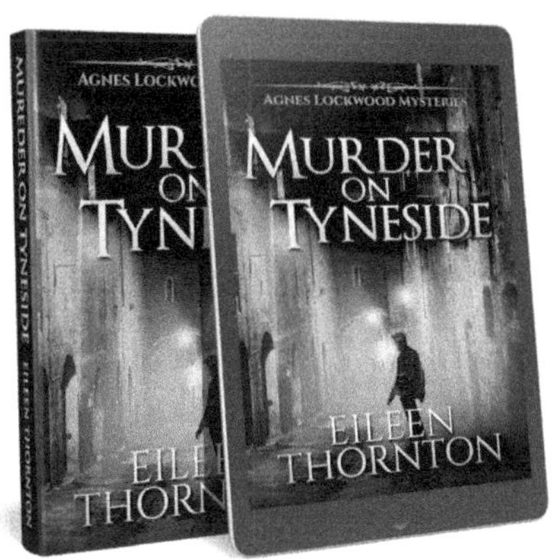

To read the first chapter for free, please head to:
https://www.nextchapter.pub/books/murder-on-tyneside-cozy-crime-mystery

CPSIA information can be obtained
at www.ICGtesting.com
Printed in the USA
LVHW011704301221
707552LV00004B/356

9 781034 417385